The Ferry Crossing

EDVARD HOEM

Translated with an Afterword by
FRANKIE DENTON SHACKELFORD

GARLAND PUBLISHING, INC.
NEW YORK & LONDON 1989

Copyright © 1989 Frankie Denton Shackelford
All Rights Reserved

Library of Congress Cataloging-in-Publication Data

Hoem, Edvard, 1949–
   [Kjærleikens ferjerciser. English]
   The Ferry Crossing/Edvard Hoem; translated with an afterword by Frankie Denton Shackelford.
         p.cm.—(The Garland Library of world literature in translation; vol. 10)
      Translation of: Kjærleikens ferjereiser.
      Includes bibliographical references.
      ISBN 0-8240-2996-8
      I. Title II. Series.
Pt9072.H57K5613   1989
839.8'3374—dc20   89-23402

Book and cover design by
Renata Gomes

Printed on acid-free, 250-year-life paper
Manufactured in the United States of America

The Ferry Crossing
Kjærleikens ferjereiser

Part one

THE FERRY CROSSING

1

He stops to buy the local newspapers from Romsdal County at a Narvesen kiosk in downtown Oslo on a rainy evening near the end of October. He takes the streetcar home to his room and sits down to read the news. He ought to be familiar with the places the papers mention, but he can't seem to find anything he recognizes in a single one of them. He looks up West Norway in an atlas; that's just as bad. Then he tears the dust-cover off his typewriter and sets to work:

For the last time!

For the very last time!

The coastline between Stad and Smøla has been tampered with! What will people think about the rest of the map? Let's correct it before it's too late.

He adds ten new nautical miles of chaotic seacoast to that area and a collection of windswept villages along the fjords reaching inland. He scatters around some islands of your average Norwegian variety and some very small ones with clusters of trees on them. Then he enters some extra routes into the network of boats run by Romsdal County and inserts a remote municipality no one has ever heard of before: Ramvik.

This is Norway, he writes.

The weather reports can deal with the wind and the rain, night and day will run their usual course. A metal stake planted in the smooth, sloping rock at the edge of the water will measure the high tide. He passes out hymnbooks to all the old women and switches on the local radio station, lights a couple of signal lanterns out in the skerries. Then he leaves the rest of the landscape in darkness while the hymns start up and the clocks tick away toward six-thirty in the evening. Is everything set now? he asks. Does everyone understand what we are talking about? We can go on;

we can go on. He is in an old house at the ferry landing on Eik Island, and just before he tugs his boots on in the dark hallway, he casts a glance behind him and sees a photograph on the wall with a handwritten signature: Christopher Bruun. Who might he have been, this fellow who allowed himself to be photographed in the prime of his life in such a serious pose? Never mind, now his inner being lives on in the feet of an older man who is walking down toward the ferry landing in a stiff wind, a man called Karl Magnus Skogmann, a supporter of the Folk High Schools, of youth in general, and of the liberal party, Venstre. He is the retired postmaster on the island, walking down in time to watch the last ferry arrival of the day. What business does he have on the other side of Eik Island Sound? None, but he likes to stand by and see which of the people coming ashore he knows and which he doesn't. He can approve whatever is arriving when he stands and watches, like he used to do with the letters that came to the island. That's Karl Magnus Skogmann stopping beneath a wind-lashed tree alongside the road to pull his hat down more firmly, for the sake of order. He can't allow anything to blow out to sea, for the wind is strong, the gray waves are slapping testily against the pilings that hold the wharf, and the thin sheets of rain are blowing past the beams of light beneath the floodlights on the ferry's loading ramp.

He becomes aware of some movement over by the shopkeeper's storage shed: a girl is sitting on a suitcase close by the wall, with the hood of her anorak pulled tight around her head and her face turned down toward the gravel. Karl Magnus Skogmann goes over and says: "Hello, Marianna, I see you're taking the ferry back to Ramvik. Got to be at work again tomorrow, I guess."

But when she doesn't answer, he goes back to his spot under the tree.

Because people may answer you when you ask them something, and then again, they may *not*. She could have answered *him*; he has known her since she was a little girl. Every step she took. He has always been there. In the darkness he can envision the head of every rusty nail in the wall behind her, and he knows the different sounds made by the corrugated tin roof above her with every shift in wind direction. He knows the sounds of people's feet as they walk along the gravel road in the dark. Just now the shopkeeper has come out and is starting to roll empty oil containers over to the loading platform and he says hello to Karl Magnus Skogmann as he goes clattering past.

Then he hears laughter over on the road and some youths appear in the light at the corner by the general store. The latest advertising posters for the Ramvik movie theater are hanging there, along with remnants of the old ones and rusty staples. The young people are crossing the sound to go to the movies and stay the night with friends.

"Well, what's showing at the Ramvik Theater this time?" the shopkeeper inquires as he goes to fetch more empty oil containers and asks what the sign posted on his store is all about.

"It's a film about Nat King Cole, but you wouldn't know anything about it," says an impudent girl whose parents are teachers, and all the others laugh. Then Karl Magnus Skogmann dares to walk over and stand there nodding toward the posters, claiming that Nat King Cole was a marvelous musician over in America. The youths laugh even more and say, "Sure, you know all about it, don't you, Skogmann."

"I do know all about it," he thinks. "I was probably the first person on this island to see a motion picture, and I was the one who worked so hard to get the circulating films shown in Ramvik. But they don't know that."

He sees by his watch that it's time for Bergen to announce the weather forecast, but the ferry still hasn't come into view on the fjord. Then he goes back over to the girl named Marianna. She is sitting where the others won't see her. He says: "There's a lecture on Wergeland in Ramvik tonight that many people would profit from hearing."

"What kind of a lecture?" she asks curtly.

And he tells her about the man who rode around on the little brown horse and says that if he were to come down toward the ferry dock on Eik Island this evening, wouldn't the horse be glistening wet and wouldn't there be water dripping from the hat of the rider sitting up there slinging flower seeds on an island off the west coast so late in October, for all the good it would do. But Karl Magnus Skogmann hears Marianna say he can go to the lecture himself if it is so important, so all he can do is follow the others into the store and seek shelter from the weather. As soon as he has gotten inside, there is a loud explosion on the far side of the island someplace, so forceful that those inside give a start and look at each other. "It's research," says the shopkeeper in such a way that everyone can hear him except Marianna,

who is sitting alone out by the storeroom wall, where the wind sends the raindrops pelting against her with each hard, quick gust. She sits motionless and does not want to go inside. The wind goes right through her anorak. She waits, expecting more loud blasts to come from out there, but all is quiet. And on top of everything, Henrik Wergeland! The cold evening clutches her chest and squeezes it; the sound of the ferry is borne in on the restless surface of the water. She thinks: "It doesn't matter, just get me away from here. Have I got my money with me?" She feels around in her purse and a warm wave washes through her body when she can't find it right off. Of course, it's there. Not much, at least not after she pays the rent, but it has never bothered her particularly if she is broke the last few days in the month. She works at a cafe and can eat whatever meals she needs there. She doesn't always need a lot. But as it is now, she wishes she had asked her father to lend her a few crowns, a fifty crown bill, since she was at home; but she couldn't have asked without his wondering why, and what could she have said then?

Now the ferry is almost docked, the captain has the engines in reverse, the loading ramp is being lowered, the teenagers start jumping on board before it's properly in place. The people who are staying on shore stretch their necks to see if there is anything of interest coming. Marianna sees the school mistress for Eik Island standing on deck, waiting to come ashore with a suitcase in each hand. When the boom is raised and she can go on board, she notices all at once that her father has come down to the docks and is standing by the loading ramp. She waves to him before she disappears down into the salon. He is standing there with the retired postmaster and she is careful to turn her face away from them, for they must not get the impression that she has been crying when they see her set her suitcase down under the overhang above the deck.

Yes, they are dynamiting on the far side of the island, day and night. That could have some effect on Marianna. There is a boat moored out there, a large, gray monster of a boat, which houses all the researchers. But soon they will no doubt have to leave on account of the weather. The ferry pulls itself away from the dock at Eik Island, and the lanterns form a pocket of light that moves across the fjord with the ferry inside it. In the salon beneath the deck the drone of the engine has become one with the boat. It is inside the walls, a rhythmic trembling, or in the rattling of a coffee cup perched unevenly on its saucer on a table. Marianna, whose last name is Kretsen, is sitting with her back to the other passengers, the teenagers on their way to the movies in Ramvik. She is not much older than they are, but they don't talk to her. A man with a ticket satchel is bending over her. She gives him the money and tucks her ticket safely behind a little plastic window in her wallet next to a picture of a friend. This is already the fifth time she has been home since vacation. She goes for her mother's sake. Always for her mother's sake. Maybe it's about time to do something for her own sake, but up to now she hasn't had the freedom to. Even though she earns the money she lives on herself. Even though they can't keep tabs on what she does in Ramvik. But they tug at her through the telephone, and she goes home to talk to her mother. They never manage to talk about anything, never. But they keep trying. This time she felt sick the whole time she was at home.

The ferry pitches in the wind that comes gusting with the rain from the port side. Above the coffee counter, which is closed now, the loudspeaker is broadcasting a station from Oslo, but it comes in poorly. Marianna looks at the abandoned coffee cup on the table there and feels as if she's going to throw up, makes her way up on deck, hangs her head over the railing and vomits.

There she stands, Marianna Kretsen. The wind and the rain make her feel better. She is eighteen years old and a waitress at the bus station in Ramvik. The buildings in the center of Ramvik are barely visible through the fog. Marianna goes down into the salon and gets her purse, locks herself in the W.C. until the boat has docked, and studies her face carefully: in a cracked and dirty mirror.

2

... If she can see herself there, all is well, he writes on that October evening. At least the mirror is in place. Before I allowed Marianna to go into the W. C. on the Eik Island ferry I had written a letter to the county boatlines and begged them to put up a mirror in there, so that the girls traveling to town can make sure their hair looks alright when they go ashore. There are so many eyes gazing steadily from behind every window since Ramvik has grown large enough to be called a *municipality*. Even when it is dark, the important thing is to *feel* that everything is in order,

now as another loud blast can be heard on the far side of the island, so that Christopher Bruun jumps a bit in his frame on the wall at Karl Magnus Skogmann's place, and the shopkeeper on the second floor of his house by the Eik Island dock looks up from the papers he is shuffling through, there in his well-lighted room and looks at the bleak, but well-lighted scene, the rain showers passing over above the watchman's shack, the ferry ramp with its hydraulic pistons, and the low storage shed. Olver Kretsen and the others have disappeared down the road. Only the school mistress is left standing there on the dock, looking uncertain what to do with her two suitcases. Skogmann is on the way to his house close by, but can't leave the area before everything is taken care of. He comes back because it appears that the teacher's husband is not there to help his wife get home. Karl Magnus turns around and goes back down to where she is standing: "Maybe you would like to leave your suitcases at my house temporarily, Henrietta? He can come for them tomorrow himself. It's no problem for me to carry them that short distance."

She opens her umbrella, he walks ahead of her, his back held straight, and soon they are there. There is a dim light coming from only one room, and the apple tree by the west wall is creaking from old age; the wind-ravaged lilac droops against the wet steps. "Come right over to the stove," he says, "it's fall now, you know."

She takes off her coat and looks around while he lights some lamps. What am I doing here, she wonders, and asks if she can use the telephone. The receiver is cold. She brushes her hair back, places it against her ear and dials the number. It occurs to her, while she listens to the ringing on the other end, that since the main switchboard is in Ramvik, her voice must go all the way over there before it comes back to the island:

"I am down at Skogmann's. My suitcases are so heavy. Can you come?"

"I didn't know you would be back before tomorrow, since the school has a holiday."

She laughs sadly: "I can't very well go back again, you know, now that the ferry has left." He pauses. "No, of course not, I'll come right away,"

but before she can say "that's fine," Skogmann calls to her from the kitchen: "You can stay a while can't you? I've put on some coffee."

"Can you come in a couple of hours? I have something I have to talk to Skogmann about."

"Which I'm not allowed to listen to," says the man. He intends this to sound like a joke, but she can just imagine his sneering expression.

"Something you can't listen to," she says. "And besides you have company."

She can hear the record player beyond him and senses that the man she calls the "friend of the family" must be there, since it's *that* record they are playing.

"Come around eleven. That will be soon enough." She hangs up. The small shivers in her body soon disappear as she sits in the chair by the hearth. She pulls off her boots and puts her feet on a low stool. Skogmann is in the kitchen getting out coffee cups and it seems so quiet in the house with all the wind outside, that he must find it appropriate to turn on the radio,

through the door he sees the nape of her neck and her hair hanging over the back of her chair, takes the coffee cups in and says that it is strange to see her sitting there, staring into the flames behind the grating on the stove,

"because that's the chair where my wife sat the last
five years of her life."

"Was she pretty, Skogmann?"

"She was a wonderful person, that's for sure."

"Was she prettier than me?"

"I don't know how to answer that . . ." He is silent for a moment before he continues. "But there was something we were going to do together, something we didn't finish with before she passed on."

"What was that?"

"I don't know what to call it."

"You must have a picture of her."

He has already poured the coffee, but she gets up anyway and goes over to the dark wooden wall, ignores Christopher Bruun hanging there, moves from one to another of the five pictures he has of Anna Martha and himself: Skogmann as a young man behind the chair she is sitting in, Skogmann and Anna Martha, each in a high-backed chair (taken by the photographer in Molde), and later on: she and Skogmann by the wall outside the house, the two of them sitting close together at a table. And then last of all: him behind the chair again, with her sitting shrunken and hunched over in it.

"You ought to remarry, Skogmann, if you are so rational that you can say, 'There was something we didn't manage to do . . .'"

"Nonsense. I am sixty years old and retired."

"Prematurely retired."

"Yes, it was wrong that the post office was shut down. I could have managed for several more years."

"It's hard to imagine what you do with your time."

"I have my books. I talk to people. Sit and look at the fjord."

"But it's no good being alone."

"No."

"Especially not getting old alone."

"No."

"Nonetheless, *I* dread going home!"

"I thought that's how you felt," says Skogmann, amazed that he can talk to her so easily,

and for the first time this evening she notices that he is looking right at her. More thundering out at sea again and he turns his eyes away, as if he had accidentally stepped in something and awkwardly moved his feet back where they had been. He says, "They are conducting research," and blows on his coffee. She looks down at her fingernails and from there to the telephone standing black and silent, and then along its lightning-fast cord that suddenly disappears into the wall. She hears the wires vibrating there under the eaves, and the apple tree thumping against the house, and here inside: his yellow fingernail as he dips down into the tobacco tin to fill his pipe. She has to walk over to the glass case where his books are. She knows he is expecting her to comment on his book collection, but she can't manage to get interested in it just at the moment. She can't find anything she can thumb through with her back to him, but she asks him if it matters to him how long she stays. His answer is bold and cheerful: "I'll keep you here as long as I can!" She laughs and says: "Thank you, Skogmann!" Then:

"Can you show me the post office?"

"It's dark and cold out there."

"That doesn't matter. I'm warm again now."

"There isn't much to see."

"I'd like to see it anyway."

And on the other side of the hallway, a naked room with shelves and a large metal cabinet. The room is partitioned by a heavy wooden counter on top of which is a brass holder filled with rubber stamps. The back room leads out toward a closed off entrance with many small square panes of glass in the door. That's where the letters came in, she thinks, and that's where they went out.

"People still get their mail even though it no longer comes through here," he says. And that is true. She runs the palm of her hand across the counter and holds it up in the light, not knowing why she has to take a stab at him this way. He pretends not to have seen it, but says stiffly:

"I try to keep things in order here."

"I never write letters," she says.

"I try to keep things in order in case they might want to use the office again."

"You really think they might?"

"No, I guess I don't really."

He turns off the light and locks up after them, hangs the keys in his bedroom where he keeps them. At that moment the telephone rings and he picks up the receiver.

"It's your husband. He wants to know if he can come and get you soon."

"Didn't I tell him eleven o'clock?"

"She says you're to come at eleven o'clock as arranged. Yes."

He hangs up and turns around. Again she says: "Thank you, Skogmann."

3

...And while they are standing there looking at each other before they go back to their chairs by the stove, the coffee in the shiny pot will have gotten cold, so that Skogmann has to be pulled up from his chair and pushed into the kitchen to turn the burner on once more. The electricity glides along the bottom of the sea in cables that have been grown over by reeds; it comes from the other side as it has done for more than a generation now—for once there were fish in the sea beyond— but it does so reluctantly these days, the man writing feels, it is as if the island had started drifting away in an ocean black as ink, and the people inside the houses he has set up were disappearing. He gropes his way along the cable on the ocean floor back to the mainland, to Ramvik, where Nat King Cole sits down at the piano on the screen in the movie theater, and plays "Careless Love," love and love, letting his fingers spread over the keyboard. The junior high school students who came on the ferry from Eik Island are catching their breath after sprinting up to the theater and getting in just under the wire. From the seats further back in the sparsely populated room one can catch glimpses of the four restless heads silhouetted against the flickering screen, against oh so careless love. Far out at sea there is a dull explosion, but the sound does not reach them in there. The theater can be placed in the west wing of a new municipal building in Ramvik. People call it the Big Cross, let's call it that,

the four wings point each in a different direction and the whole building has become a heavy cross for Ramvik to bear. But also a monument to its era, a landmark for the boats that go across Ramvik Sound between Eik Island and the mainland, an example for other large towns, and a lifelong project that has passed out of the hands of the architect, the man who pencilled in the horizon on his drawing and saw the wings of the building lift themselves like enormous bird-wings and raise the whole complex up from the sea. The autumn rain on this evening beats against the copper on the outer walls, there are lights on here and there in the conference rooms on the floors above, the box office employee changes the posters by the ticket window while the evening's performance is still in full swing. This is the heart of Ramvik. It is here the various governmental and social agencies are moving in, one by one as their offices are furnished and made ready, and it is here

THE FERRY CROSSING

people can come with most of the burdens of daily life. Income tax forms are on a counter at the main entrance and at the post office a window is open until late in the evening. The fishing boats out at sea never stop calling the telephone operators on their radios, and the adult education office never stops inviting everyone to learn any languages they don't yet know. Next to this colossus is a smaller building: the Bus Station Cafe, where there are
a couple of hours until closing time, practically no customers, a radio on in the kitchen. But there's someone shouting for Metta Nilsen, who is alone on duty. She has been gone for a while now and people are wondering where she can be,

when she comes running in from the bus where she was checking on a package, she explains, containing newspapers she was expecting, but it didn't come. She wonders why they haven't arrived. They should have been there. But it might be that the plane didn't manage to take off in time from Fornebu Airport in Oslo, or maybe there was some problem at a dirty building down by the Aker River where Metta Nilsen's pile of newspapers should have started their journey. That's where they should have started, with

their vision of a different country, with their theories about how this country would look, and what it should be like, there at the fingertips of a young man at an address machine, who might have wondered for a moment: where the hell is Ramvik? before he loaded the package along with many others into a delivery truck and rushed off toward the airport, theories, theories, even a theory for a masthead on their little rag: The Class Struggle, what does that mean? Never mind, up in the air, over the mountains, and down on a fog-covered strip of asphalt near a town in western Norway, and lots of other places as well, onto busses and trucks, until it finally should have arrived on the bus to Ramvik, addressed to Metta Nilsen. It didn't arrive this evening. She serves the customers who are waiting and afterwards goes over to talk with a bus driver who is sitting by the window looking out at the fjord and the darkness. Another driver, the one whose bus just arrived, comes up the stairs and sees her lips moving through the glass door, but doesn't hear what she is saying, and she stops when he comes in: "It must be the new uniform that makes the difference," he says to her as he sits down. It has always been like that with uniforms and girls: "Can you get me some coffee, Metta, and make it quick. I've got to leave again right away."

"You call that a uniform?" Metta comes balancing the coffee cup, casts a glance around the room, relights the butt of her cigarette and perches on the edge of a table close by them. "Don't you want any money for the coffee," they ask her. She shakes her head and says, "Shhh, I didn't ring it up. Once in a while I have to cheat the company out of half a crown, otherwise it just isn't worth it." The fellow pouring down the coffee says that's the way those communists are. You can't trust them. But the coffee's good, and maybe it's a special deal, a free cup after you buy a certain number. They get into a heated discussion about whether it is the coffee drinking or the swing shifts that make you feel you're developing an ulcer, until the girl in the kitchen comes in and says that they ought not to shout like that. Do they think they own the whole cafe or what? "No," says the guy drinking the free coffee, and all three of them laugh,

while the bus stands out at the bus stop, waiting for them all to head in different directions,

and Marianna Kretsen comes from the Eik Island ferry and crosses the road with a suitcase in one hand. She looks around and wonders for a moment if she has enough money to take a taxi so she won't get soaking wet, but there isn't one available at the station, so she walks up between the Big Cross and the Bus Station Cafe, and then left toward Langfot Street where she has a room. Metta Nilsen sees her between the buildings from the cafe window, opens it out into the rain and calls down to her: "Marianna!" But she doesn't hear her, and disappears around the corner. Metta closes the window,

wondering why Marianna didn't come up. When she comes back from a visit at home she usually comes racing up the stairs to the cafe to talk, sits down and has a smoke as if she needs to rest after a hard job, and Metta has gotten into the habit of saying: "So you got away again this time, too?"

"Just barely." And they tell each other what has happened since they saw each other last. This time she didn't come,

the bus drivers leave, Metta Nilsen sits down behind the counter with a newspaper, but can't concentrate on what she's reading. After a customer has come in and she has served him, she just stands there, leaning on the glass counter for a long time, staring out into the room. As usual on those evenings she has the late shift, she gets more and more impatient as the hours go by. She looks at the clock time and time again: they could just as well be closed, as few customers as come at this time, and there is nothing left of the evening when she gets off as late as ten o'clock. Not that there is so awfully much to do anyway. Ramvik is not a very big place, and when fall comes, it's all over—for a girl of eighteen who works at the cafe. Those who feel like reading books go to the library in the Big Cross and borrow one. Those who go to schools other than the high school leave town. The younger members of the town government continue to exchange visits within their own little select group, and the religious types turn on the heat at the mission house. Metta Nilsen has headquarters quite near them, a room in the attic of a run-down public building, where a handful of people meet once a week or so, to look at papers sent from an unknown address in Oslo. They work hard to keep alcoholic beverages out of the attic meetings, and usually they are successful. They make up Ramvik's little hardcore of communists, which doesn't seem likely to amount to much. They have not gotten any new members for the last half year and a study group at the high school has evaporated into nothing

so that's why Metta Nilsen feels, as she walks past the mission house on her way to one of many shivering cold meetings, that she envies those people sitting inside there, playing the guitar: there are a lot of them. They are secure, they keep up with each other as the years go by, through youth groups and old folks' groups and children's groups. They follow a well-worn path onward, and it is clear as crystal for them that the world is evil, but God is good, everything that can be explained is O.K. and everything that can't be is O.K. too, a miracle is a miracle, and the scripture they adhere to is impossible to get lost in, but rather divided up and numbered in convenient little pieces you can take in and mull over and enjoy, and

isn't the movie over yet? She walks to the window again and looks down, but it's deserted outside the theater where the posters hang. The rain is pouring down, she can see it in the circles of light beneath the street lamps, and she stands there looking at all the wetness, until she finally realizes that she takes a certain pleasure in torturing herself with thoughts of how gray and dreary this winter in Ramvik is going to be.

She looks at the clock again. Everything is tidy, there isn't a single soul in the cafe. She clenches her teeth tightly and quickly sucks in some air, starts making noise with the cups behind the counter, and drops a crown in the jukebox just to . . . just to make the time pass! No other reason.

. . . You know, thinks the man who is writing this in Oslo, that may be just how it is. The world won't allow itself to be played in reverse, the needle moves imperceptibly, but inexorably toward the center, a click and then it is silent, no use saying any more about it, that would be like sitting in a movie theater and putting up a protest when the show is over: "I refuse to accept that it's over!" Or like an attempt to escape through the seven glass cheese bells, if you will, as a child does when he writes his name in a book: Ramvik, Romsdal County, Norway, Europe, The Earth, The Solar System, The Milky Way Galaxy, the attempt to find oneself by grabbing the Universe by the tail. At any rate he now writes that

4

Marianna Kretsen from Eik Island comes crawling back to her private existence and stands with water dripping off her in front of the door to the basement of the building she lives in. She has to unlock two different doors to get in. It is cold there in the subterranean cement tunnel that leads to her room. From the floor above she can smell dinner, even though it is quite late, a repugnant smell of gravy or fried meat that lingers, wafting through the damp air. She goes into her room. The little battery-operated radio crackles and sputters when she turns it on to find some of the music that is always out there in the air. She is not scared, not nauseated any longer. At the sink she squeezes the water out of her hair, dries it with a towel, and runs a comb through it. In the mirror she studies her face again and lets the weather take the blame for the way she looks. She is not in any real pain; her nipples just feel a bit sore. She thinks: "Food, I've got to eat something." But in the cupboard there are only a couple of thin wieners she doesn't feel like eating. The mere thought of the pearls of grease that form in the water wieners have been boiled in is enough to make her gag. Careful now. She turns up the electric heat, settles into the couch with a blanket over her, and waits.

Waits??

Back when she stumbled across this room for rent she was thrilled to have a little private space. She had never lived alone before, never had a room of her own. All through her childhood at home on Eik Island there had always been a crib or child's bed in the room where she slept, with one of her two siblings in it, small tots who cried early on cold winter mornings before she left for school. Mom would come still reeling with sleep to carry them down to the first floor where the stoves were lighted,

and later she went to the Folk High School, that big white house over on the hill she remembers so well, the bus driving off in a cloud of dust, her walking slowly up the well maintained path to the house, to the freshly scrubbed, flower bedecked rooms—so proper that it makes you ache. She has to share the room with two other girls; she has never shared a room with anyone her own age before,

so the first few evenings she gets undressed and creeps under the covers before the others come up, afraid that they will see her body and maybe have some opinion about it. It's on account of

her mother, who is on Eik Island, that she feels embarrassed: never go naked where the children will see it. Regardless of how crowded they were, she had never seen an inch of her mother's body without having the feeling of doing something wrong,

and one night when she was about ten years old and woke up, scared because it was dark outside and dark in the room where she was sleeping, she goes into her parents' room, and they've fallen asleep with the light on and are lying so close to each other in the narrow bed. The covers have slid off, but they don't notice the cold. They are sleeping: her mother with her hands up above her head, her nightgown rolled up beneath her armpits, her father stark naked and curled up against her. Nothing in the world will ever get Marianna to go into their room at night again. But here!

on Langfot Road in Ramvik she has sort of moved into a more spacious body. The real Marianna no longer needs to stay inside her skin and her clothes, now that she has gotten a room of her own. Her mother was against it, it wasn't really necessary at all, she could work it out so she only had early shifts at the cafe if she wanted to, and then the Eik Island ferry would fit nicely into her schedule, but her father

looks strangely out of the window, straight through the curtains, and says: "Of course you should move, if you want to and can pay for it . . ."

The evening she moves in Metta helps her carry things up from the dock. She has carefully thought out where to put everything. There was already a couch, a table and chair there. She hammers big nails into the walls out of sheer joy, never once thinking that the landlord might disapprove, and hangs her things up. Metta has to go,

Marianna pulls the shades, locks the door, turns the radio on full blast, takes off every bit of her clothing, hops around naked on what little bit of floor space there is until the whole room is filled with nothing but Marianna, who keeps hopping around on the floor and up on the couch, this

couch she is sitting on now, on an evening in the month of October (waiting). Bit by bit she becomes warm as toast: first her cheeks start to burn while her hair still feels wet and cold on the back of her neck, then the warmth surges through her whole body, like faint chills at first, and later on like a wave of heat, and she gets heavy and sleepy despite the hunger gnawing inside her. Yes?

There is someone knocking at the door. Telephone for you, Marianna. She gets scared again, as if she has done something wrong and been caught, can't imagine who can be calling, hurries upstairs. Oh. How are you, Marianna? Her mother is talking from the other side of Eik Island Sound. Father thought so, too . . . I thought . . . (Couldn't he keep it to himself? Did he see that I was crying at the dock?) "It's just my period, Mamma. I have cramps." It occurs to her that she has never talked to her mother about such things, but the lie slid easily off her tongue. "I'm going to work tomorrow. Of course, I am. It's not that bad. No."

"I didn't know that you usually got sick," her mother said and kept talking and talking. She'll have to quit soon. The connection is poor. "I'll send a space heater with your father. It gets so cold in the basement." "That's not necessary, Mamma."

"Go to bed now. Then you'll be rested up by tomorrow. Yes. Bye-bye." Marianna manages to hang up and thank them for the use of the telephone. The man of the house stares at her: "You aren't sick, are you?

You look a bit . . ."

"I was soaked when I got here."

He asks if she needs anything. All she has to do is ask. She thanks him.

Back down in her room she sits down on the couch again, picks up a book, tries to read, but can't, lies back to see if she feels tired enough to sleep, but she isn't. Bit by bit the dilemma from earlier in the day comes back to her, the call she made from her home to a doctor's office in Ramvik, the clear voice of the nurse on the telephone, smooth and crisp like the uniforms they wear, those women: *It's out of the question for this doctor. Ask the social services consultant at the Big Cross to help you find another one.* If I can stand this until tomorrow, I'll try to figure something out. She decides to take it easy, but can't, looks at the clock and sees it's another half hour before Metta gets off work. She puts on her anorak which is wringing wet. It is still raining outside. She doesn't have an umbrella, but hurries, running through the showers down to the Bus Station Cafe in downtown Ramvik, a hunched over, dark creature dashing past the large, bright window panes in the Big Cross, where the movie posters hang.

5

The man writing this has gone out into the October evening to get some air. He wanders up Bygdøy Avenue and sees people coming out of the theater. So he lets the movie in Ramvik be over, too, and empties the theater in the Big Cross. Careless, worthless love. But the lecture on Wergeland upstairs can last a while longer.

Over on Eik Island Olver Kretsen has come from the ferry dock in the pouring rain. In the darkness the sheep drift away from the flat stony ridges on the far side of the island, and group themselves in clumps of wet wool in a cleft in the rock or cower against a wall for shelter from the weather, as Olver Kretsen comes to his house up the road with big lumps of gravel and soil hanging on the back of his boots and knocks them off out in the entryway, where his eyes disappear facing the light in the ceiling. He comes into the kitchen, sits down on a chair by the radio, lights his pipe, waits for the warmth,

and his wife asks him if he saw Marianna down by the docks, and if he noticed that she was different than usual. He says: "She might have been . . ." "You noticed it, too!" cries his wife. "It's not just my nerves!"

He looks through the newspaper. Follows the columns up and down, reads quickly, and once in a while looks over at the woman he is married to. She is standing at the sink washing dishes, moving them here and there with small jerks. She is endlessly slow at it. When he was walking down toward the docks she was also standing there washing dishes. She can turn a dish washing into a full day's work, he thinks, at least when anyone is watching her.

Here they are, under their own roof, the slate roof he put on this summer, twenty years after he settled down here. When the slates are in place you might say it is finished, this adventure he set out on thirty-five years ago when he worked his way west from one construction job to the next (from a spot east of the mountains) and at a government work project in Ramvik came across the father of the woman now standing there. Won't she ever get done washing those dishes? That was after the Norwegian Labor Party had come into power and established a government work program so that people would get a chance to use their bodies . . .

and the woman standing there at the sink interrupts his train of thought and asks:

"Should we maybe call and ask Marianna how she's doing?"

Anna-Marja will never finish washing dishes, just keeps standing there rubbing a glass as if there were something wrong with it.

"We should in any case wait until she gets to Ramvik."

"That's what I meant, Olver."

"Of course."

He keeps paging through the newspaper, a newspaper from that part of the country he comes from originally, but there is less and less of interest in it,

THE FERRY CROSSING

he is very familiar with the names of the places they write about: *that* town! it's only two and a half kilometers from downtown. But the people, the ones worth writing about back east, he knows nothing about as a rule, not any more. That's all changed now. The ones he grew up with seldom appear in the headlines; that wasn't for *them*, careers and positions and publicity. Once in a while he sees them in the obituaries. Most of them are surely still living, but they crawled into the mine shafts long ago, and disappeared there . . .

"There can't be anything wrong in calling and asking how she's doing."

"No, that's perfectly o.k., I should think."

"But we have to wait until she has gotten to her room. We can't call before that."

"That's what I've been saying," he answers,

while she stands there rubbing and holding the glass up toward the light, never finishing. The same pathological pedantry her father had, that man who

came to work on the government work project and got in the way of the others for one crown and fifty öre a day, talked to God often enough, called himself "citizen" and held lectures during the lunch breaks against socialism and tyranny and in favor of private property and personal liberty, had his own little farm, but was always quick to make extra money for work he didn't do. Everyone laughed at him and everyone listened to him. And because he never got anything done, it was said that he was steady and dependable. His head was full of ideas about how the world should be saved before it was too late and controlled by communism and dictatorship. Then he went to a convention of the Samfund Party and came back worse than ever. Then the bicycle that was Ramvik Township got a puncture in both of its tires and was placed under public administration a few years before the war, and Citizen Sivert—he considered the designation an honor—was appointed supervisor by the government, in charge of seeing that the chaos of left-wingers in the township didn't make a bigger mess than it already had. He was so meticulous that nothing was accomplished before he, to his own astonishment, succumbed to pneumonia just before Christmas a few years later, and

"She ought to be there now, don't you think?" He sees that Anna-Marja's eyes are glued to the clock above the cabinet:

"What?"

"I said that Marianna must be at her room by now."

"It takes her a quarter of an hour to walk up from the ferry, you know."

"Still, she ought to be there pretty soon now."

"We'd better wait until around eight-thirty, Anna-Marja."

She isn't like that, he thinks; Anna-Marja is *not* like that. She *wasn't* that way when he met her

on the bit of road over in Ramvik where he and her father are standing, shooting the breeze with each other while they lay the rockwork for a little bridge over a stream, and they stop and look out into Eik Island Sound because a rowboat is coming from over there. Citizen Sivert grabs his binoculars and drops everything else, as usual: "That's Anna-Marja bringing me the lunch I left at home." It happens again and again. They stand there silently while she talks to her father and rows back. They watch her and mumble quietly among themselves and ask, when she has left, how much Citizen Sivert wants for her, a good bit most likely, and he curses over their unchristian talk, but forgets to take his lunch several more times, so his daughter keeps having to bring it and sit there with them during the lunch break,

"It's well past eight, Olver."

"We better wait a little longer."

"Sure hope her landlord and his wife don't go to bed early."

"It is completely acceptable behavior to call before ten p.m., Anna-Marja." And he has to smile because he thinks about

her standing there bent over the lunch basket, and him being unable to control himself, sneaking up behind her and slipping a worm down the neck of her blouse and the whole crew storming over to help get it out amidst torrents of laughter and noise-making. A little later, when the food break is over, he is down by the river bed to pick up some gravel, and she grabs a bucket of water standing next to the cement mixture and pours it down his back and runs for all she's worth to the boat, jumps in and rows away

he hears the guffaws rising sky high from the twelve men in the work crew: "That cooled you off!" "How does it feel to be in your pants after that one?"

a few more comments and he tosses what he is holding, runs after her, and finds a boat a bit further away. She is rowing for her life with him after her, churning the water to foam. Far out in the fjord he overtakes her.

"By God, if he didn't catch her," he heard Citizen Sivert had said, with satisfaction. And later on Sivert turned to Olver and announced: "The next thing you know she'll be coming over here with your lunch," happy as he was to be rid of the burden of providing for her, and Olver replied, "That just might be." "She's full of smallfry," shouted one of the guys who had trouble keeping his mouth shut, "she's full of communist smallfry!" Citizen Sivert sputters: "Suffer the little children to come unto me. I'll take the hellion out of them!"

"I think we must be out of hot water, Olver."

"Oh, probably, that tank doesn't hold much . . ."

She stands there turning the faucet on and off, but there isn't any more. He sits with his newspaper, reading and not reading. She turns and looks at him and he feels that she is trying to get him to look at the clock. Silently he grumbles that

she isn't *like* that, she's just gotten that way by virtue of having bustled around this kitchen for more than twenty years, and it's an accusation at himself, but she has never come out and said that she wanted to leave and so, of course, he couldn't just

where would they have gone? There has never been any prospect of giving her any other lifestyle. He feels he has done what he could, been nice to her, always done what she asked of him, and in recent years, as she has become more and more difficult to deal with, he has humored her, said what she wanted to hear, just to keep peace in the family, thinking: it is a difficult age for a woman, and I have no business making it worse for her, and

that's how things came to a halt between them.

she looks at him again, and gives a thousand little signals so he will understand that now they simply *have* to call, he tries to remain quiet for a while yet, but can't do it, he has to get up, walks out into the hallway and says: "O.K., we may as well call now."

She follows him and says: "Maybe they won't like us calling, her landlords I mean. Maybe they'll give her a hard time if we bother them. Shouldn't we wait until tomorrow instead and see . . ."

He knows that they have to call or the night will be intolerable.

"You dial the number, Olver."

"O.K., I'm looking for it."

His hands have difficulty with the thin pages in the telephone book, but he finds what he is looking for at last, dials, hears someone answer right away, and asks for Marianna. Anna-Marja trembles as she reaches for the receiver he is handing to her and whispers:

"Maybe we ought to write that number down, Olver, so we have it next time."

Now Marianna has come to the phone and he can just barely hear, standing there as close to his wife as possible, that she is saying "hello" far away. The connection is bad with a lot of crackling and static, but he manages to catch "It's just menstruation, Mamma,"

and for a long time after Marianna has hung up, Anna-Marja Kretsen sits holding the black receiver to her ear. But there's no one there and she finally hangs up and says:

"It's just menstrual cramps, Olver."

"I could hear that's what she said."

"I've never been bothered by that myself."

"It must vary from woman to woman . . ."

"If she had just stayed put here until tomorrow, we could have avoided making that call."

"At least it wasn't anything serious."

"But it seems like she doesn't want to be around us and doesn't stay at home any longer than she has to."

"I think Marianna is very good about coming home."

"She's up to something we don't know about."

"Well, and why shouldn't she be?"

He goes into the kitchen and gathers up the newspaper he abandoned. She asks a couple of times what he meant by that. He's never said anything like that before, but

he just reads in silence, and she watches him quite a while before she turns around to try to finish the dishes on the counter

the kitchen counter I got Olver Kretsen to build, says the man writing—a good kitchen counter in his house out there on the island I made. I didn't make it any bigger than necessary. Big enough to be included on the map after this. A medium-sized island, maybe one and a half kilometers long, with a stubby road flung in between the rocky knolls, a strip rolled out with a flick of the wrist. Beyond it he lets some reefs and sandbars stick up out of the sea. From the mainland they perceive the island as a heavy, dark blotch on the horizon at dusk, and a haphazard collection of luminous dots when the darkness comes. But on autumn mornings, when it clears up, the island unfurls like a cheery sail on the ocean of sky with the sun glowing red through the heather and the premature frost. The blows of a hammer down by the docks can be heard straight across the sound, as the ferry comes silently through the water with its white wreath of foam around the stern: Eik Island-Ramvik, Norway. There's Olver Kretsen standing on the front deck as usual, with that flat, brown briefcase of his under his arm. He curls the ticket between his fingertips in his pocket and looks inward toward the day he faces. Always standing with his feet spaced wide, as if he needed to brace himself for a rough sea, always impatient to go ashore, as if standing so far in the bow of the boat would help

but this evening. He hears yet another blast from the far side of the island, the floor planks dip imperceptibly beneath him at that moment, and his wife asks once again: "What's that?" "It's research," he says, to give her some sort of an answer. He gets a rag, wipes up the dish water spilled on the floor so that she won't keep tracking through it all night. She has sat down on a chair and is looking dully out the kitchen window.

6

Metta Nilsen moves around the Bus Station Cafe in Ramvik, cleaning up for the night. She stacks the chairs up so that the cleaning lady can get around more easily. A boy's pale face appears at the door. Metta tells him to go away; the cafe is already closed. That is not quite true perhaps, but she figures the whole group of movie-goers is close on his heels and she can't bear to let them all in. But he says, "There's someone outside who wants to talk to you," and disappears back down the stairs. "Can't they come up here if they want to talk to me so badly?" she calls after him, but he is already gone.

At first she thinks it's just something they've come up with to irritate her, that gang of youths which often gathers outside the cafe in the evenings, because there is an overhanging roof that protects them from the rain, because there is a hot dog stand nearby, and because there is nothing to do in the evenings in Ramvik. But immediately afterwards Metta goes down anyway, pretending that she is going to lock the outer door to avoid having a lot of traffic on the stairs, now that the cafe is closing anyway. She shivers as she steps out on the landing. In order to get warm she allows herself to slide down the bannister, and the coarse cloth in the dirndl skirt that is the uniform in this idiotic establishment makes her sail briskly around the sudden turns in the staircase on the way down. She sees no one outside and is about to slam the door shut when

Marianna Kretsen comes creeping around the corner like a little, black, wet animal and asks: "Can you wait a minute, Metta? Has Mrs. Haugen gone?"

She drags Marianna with her up to the kitchen, and there, by the counter where the orders are prepared at the Bus Station Cafe, Marianna tells what she has found out in a telephone conversation from her home to a doctor earlier that day: that a pregnancy test was positive, now, of all times, when it's all over with that guy named Hans. She looks at Metta without moving, as if she were glued to the chair, just sits there with a straight back, pressing her palms together and says softly: "What'll I do?"

Metta Nilsen goes around locking doors and turning off lights. There are no curtains in that kitchen; people can look right in at them from the houses across the street. She leaves a single lightbulb burning above the counter where they are sitting with their chairs right up to it. She gets out some sandwich rolls and wants to force Marianna to eat, but instead Marianna jumps up and out to the W.C. where she stands gagging above the enameled toilet bowl, but can't get anything up. Her skin is cold and damp, but still she is sweating.

Metta: "You've told Hans about this?"
"No, and I don't know if I will either."
"He ought to have to take his share of the responsibility."
"I don't want to have him back on account of this."
"No, but he ought to help you. I'll call him."
"O.K., but not tonight. It's too late."
"For who?"
"His landlords don't like people calling so late. They've said so."
"I don't give a damn about that."

"But do you think it's right to get him involved in this?"

"Do you think you can deal with it by yourself?

Marianna says: "No, I thought so, but now I don't think so any more," and suddenly she feels dead-tired, ready to fall asleep right where she is, puts her head down on the counter in front of her, empty and sleepy, doesn't even feel like crying. Metta lights a cigarette and goes over to the window before she turns around and says: "I'm going to call him right away."

"Do whatever you want. I can't take any more," says Marianna.

Metta takes the phone book off the wall and starts paging through it, mumbling the alphabet as if she were swearing beneath her breath, until she finds the number and then repeats it to herself as she walks over to the entrance where the telephone is hanging. She says: "Hello. Excuse me for calling so late, but I must speak with Hans Kristiansson," and she sees Marianna slumped there beneath the solitary lightbulb, while she stands quietly cursing and waiting for Hans Kristiansson to come to the phone.

7

The man writing this has gone back to his room and is trying to straighten out the map. Right out there is where the island is supposed to be. Maybe you can't see it in the dark, with its stubby road running between the small houses and the tree clusters, the rocky knolls, the patches of field and the heather. There, at the northernmost point, it stops, up against a pile of rock and a clump of stubborn, wind-lashed trees. After that, the ocean. Right next to that rocky knoll, protected from the worst of the weather, lies the house where Henrietta Brunberg lives, along with her husband,

the man who is standing there now with the receiver gone dead in his hand after Henrietta has hung up down at Skogmann's. It is late October, he has made a fire in the fireplace, and next to it sits another man tapping his foot in time with the record player. Arve Brunberg, the teacher's husband, looks at the telephone receiver once more before he slams it back on the hook and, amazed that he dares to act so impulsively, keeps standing at the window, looking at the miserable, rainy weather that you can never get away from on this miserable island. Who in the hell would have thought that this weather was the only kind available in these parts? He looks at the other fellow, intending to say something, but he appears to be inaccessible for conversation, tapping his foot and humming lethargically with the record playing: "I can see it in your eyes. You're not here."

Arve Brunberg says: "I have half a bottle left. We might as well finish it off." At that the great mane of hair over there comes to life and nods thoughtfully. Arve Brunberg goes to the kitchen to get some glasses. After a couple of shots the guest comes to and becomes aware of the room he is sitting in. "Weren't you supposed to go after Henrietta?"

"Skogmann won't let me. They won't be finished until eleven o'clock."

"Finished with what?"

"Surely I don't have to spell it out for you."

"Come on now. The man is well over sixty."

"Oh, Henrietta probably just finds that exciting. The idea is to experiment, if you are a woman out looking for the great liberation."

"It must be nerve wracking around this place these days."

"You better believe it!"

"You aren't losing your grasp on things, are you?"

"It would take a hell of a guy to satisfy her, the way she's gotten lately."

"Here's to women, Arve!"

"Here's to women!"

So they sit there drinking and lolling away the evening with Arve knowing full well that the guest is just waiting around to see what will happen when Henrietta comes home, but neither of them mentions her again. For long periods of time nothing can be heard but the playing cards as they are slapped onto the table or come whizzing from under the dealer's thumb, the record player mumbling at the other end of the room that "I can see it in your eyes," and the foot of the guest, the one Henrietta calls the friend of the family, tapping in time to the music. Finally when they have guzzled enough booze, those gentlemen, so that they can get really chummy with each other, the friend of the family tells a story about a chick working in the mess hall on a boat he was on once, who managed to wreck the whole atmosphere on board and Arve Brunberg says that he can imagine that easily. But, nonetheless, the guest says that the sailor's life is the only real life, and Brunberg says so true, so true, though he has never been beyond the skerries in his life. But he's just answering absent-mindedly, for he is already caught up in his own story, the one he starts telling now about the time when

he and Henrietta are at a party at the home of some people they know in Ramvik on the other side of the sound. Henrietta is in a mood he has never seen her in before. It is in the summertime that this happens, with an outdoor staircase leading to a little garden, where Henrietta sits the whole evening talking with one of the men at the party, while he himself walks around aimlessly, incapable of getting into a conversation with any of the people laughing and flitting around him, but he hears them talking about Henrietta and how she is always such fun to be with. He has held out until a little past midnight and he is sitting all alone in a chair, having turned everyone away for quite some time, when Henrietta suddenly comes over to him and asks: "There isn't anything wrong, is there, Arve?"

He looks at the hectic blush on her cheeks. He knows that either they had better get out of there or he is going to hit her. He says he has such an unbearable headache and would prefer to go home as soon as possible, but that she can, of course, stay there until the next day. Of course, she can. She sits down next to him, fiddles with her bracelet, sticking her finger through it while she says out loud to herself: "Why not? Sure, why not?" But when he gets his things and gets ready to leave, so furious he is nearly in tears, she has decided that she wants to go with him after all. Going home in the boat on the small waves in the summer night, still light enough so they can see each other well, a light wind, Henrietta up in the bow, him at the back, steering. The drone of the motor is powerful and pleasant, giving them an excuse not to talk to each other. There she sits with the wind ruffling her hair. The vibrations in the boat creep over into his body and he keeps trembling after they have gone ashore on Eik Island and walk in silence up to the house where they live. The bedroom on the second floor is filled with the sweet and strong scent of summer blossoms in a vase. He sees Henrietta once again as she was at the party and the vision fills him with desire for her, and he throws himself on top of her and wants to force his way inside her, as if it were years since he had seen her last, and as if he had scarcely managed to bear it. She doesn't reject him immediately. But after a little while she breaks it off, pushes him away, stands up in the gray light of the northern summer night and says: "This is what I would call rape and I won't let you go through with it." She leaves the room and lying there alone he hears her go into the guest room, lock the door behind her and lie down on the bed there.

"What do you think of that one?"

What do you think of that one?

The guest leans back in his chair and blows smoke rings up toward the ceiling. Over in the corner the record player is doing its thing. Arve Brunberg walks over to the window and looks at the rain coming down through the outdoor light and every second it is as if he sees something moving at the periphery of the circle, but it isn't her. He says: "And here. Here's where Henrietta stood for half an hour the first day we came to the island. The moving crates, everything we had with us was lying in a pile on the floor. I'm standing in the big middle of it, sweating and unpacking, but Henrietta! She's standing like a statue in the middle of the floor, not giving a damn about putting things away, though we knew we would be visited by the old teacher that same evening. She just stands there looking out through the window.

"Finally I say to her: 'Don't you have any intention of helping me unpack? Did you think I was planning to do it all alone?'

"That's when she says, without even turning around:

'I thought you said we could see the water from the parlor window, the actual ocean, I mean, but that isn't true at all.'

"'I never said that,' I say, 'you can see the ocean from the window on the second floor.'

"'But that's not the same thing. I thought I'd be able to see it from here,' she says and turns around slowly. This, too, is an attack on me. It's my fault the house is built in such a way that one cannot see the ocean from the first floor! What do you think of that? What does the ocean have to do with all this? What does Henrietta have to do with the ocean? Answer me that, will you?"

Hasn't got any more reason to be on this island than Henrietta does, the man writing this notes, and lets Arve Brunberg slowly sink his weight into a chair and remain there as the guest puts on his overcoat and makes his way out into the wind. Never even wanted to have anything to do with the folks on the island, talks to them, but never gets involved in their affairs, has an island on the island to come home to when the ferry from Ramvik docks late in the afternoon carrying those people who have been across the sound at work, straight home to take care of Henrietta, until she won't let herself be taken care of any more, poor plant, doesn't get enough air. He sits there and waits for her this evening. Everything is wide open, but she doesn't want to come. Sooner or later she'll *have* to, and he knows that. She can't move in with Skogmann for good. She has to creep out into the foul weather and drift on home, past the house where Olver Kretsen lives,

where Olver is lying in the dark in the bedroom up in the loft, close enough to his wife, Anna-Marja, so he can reach out his hand and touch her. It has always been Olver who has had to make the first move if they are to touch each other. That's how it used to be, but now he doesn't do it any more for they are surely not . . .

She knows he is lying over there in the dark, listening to the rain on the new slate roof, the one that will last his lifetime. They have managed to get to bed this night, like all the others, by him helping her, as usual, with everything she thinks ought to be done, everything she can't leave as it is, the floor that has to be wiped up just one more time, checking twice to see that the electricity is turned off, that the two boys are sleeping safely in their beds downstairs. Olver knows it has all been taken care of already, and she knows it, but still she can't get to sleep. What if the door isn't locked down there? (She knows it is; he knows it is.) It must be the salty food that makes my mouth so dry, she thinks. I can't tolerate salty food. I'm thirsty and I don't have anything to drink, not here. She feels the cotton tongue in her mouth and sooner or later she *has* to have something to drink or she'll never fall asleep. But *he* needs to sleep now. He has to get up around six the next morning, and if she goes down to get something to drink now, it will be a long time before she's back up there again, and the thought of him lying there awake can make her want to stay down in the kitchen in hopes that he will have gone to sleep before she gets back. Now she thinks: Maybe he'll fall asleep soon. Then I can go down and stay there as long as I need to, her thirst is growing stronger. She has to turn over in bed. She knows that he won't fall asleep for a while yet for she notices that he is lying on his back with the palms of his hands supporting his head, not on his side as he always does when he falls asleep:

"Olver, are you sure the door is locked?"

"That's the last thing I did before we came up."

"Oh, well then it must be."

But she's thinking: Can there be anything else that wasn't done, like maybe...

then he sits up in bed and she hears him say: "My mouth is so dry, I'm going down and get a drink of water. Want me to bring you something, too?"

"Since you're going anyway, bring me a little water."

He lights a lamp on the wall and goes downstairs. She hears the tap running in the kitchen and fumbles with her hand in the drawer of the night stand, finds a little bottle which she opens with trembling hands, takes out the cotton plug and puts the tablet into her mouth. Get rid of the bottle, he's already on the stairs. She tries to lie quietly, with the tablet in the corner of her mouth. He gives her the glass; she puts it up to her mouth. It feels like sand on her lips but she gets the water down. A little later a numbness spreads over her throat and helps her breathing blend into his. A small sigh and he's out. And still she can hear the rain on the slate roof, but it's growing fainter; she notices a light pressure against her temples and grows lethargic, it will be here soon, a tinkling bell far away,

8

and a telephone ringing in the entry way of a house on the outskirts of Ramvik—the man writing this hears it—a woman's hand picks up the receiver, and right afterwards goes over and knocks on a door. When the door is opened they see her, the people who are in the room, some friends playing cards at a table: it's the landlady of one of them, coughing demonstratively at the clouds of smoke and saying: "Hans Kristiansson, there's a telephone call for you." He jumps up. Reaching the phone he hears that it is Metta Nilsen saying that he has to come as soon as possible to Marianna's, and he thinks he knows what this is all about. His bicycle light isn't working; he has to pedal in toward the center of Ramvik in the pitch darkness. A little ways up Langfot Road he swerves off the road, abandons the bike and jogs the final meters up to the house. Metta opens the door and says: "It's a good thing you came." Inside the room it is so bright that he can't see at first, but there's only Marianna sitting there on the divan with a blanket around her. She doesn't smile when he comes in. Metta sits with them for a while and then gets up suddenly and disappears.

There is silence between the two who are left. He wonders what he is going to say. What she wants to say. He finds himself falling into the usual pattern without wanting to, listening to the alarm clock ticking, the cars and all the traffic passing by outside, until Marianna suddenly lays her head down in his lap and says: "We don't have to talk about it now, but could you not go home? I want you to be here with me." There is only one thing to do. They pull off their clothes and snuggle down close to each other under the comforter on the narrow divan. She tries to find a spot for her damp head on his shoulder. After a while he starts feeling warm, with the thin, girlish body pressed up against him so there'll be room for them both. He hasn't got any great ideas, but he'll figure out some way to help her for sure: He runs his hand gently up along her body, touches one of her nipples. She looks at him strangely out of one eye; he clears his throat: "Since you're already . . . we might just as well . . ." But at that her eyes open wide and she says: "Don't you understand anything?" She quickly turns her back to him and he lies there stiff as a board until they finally fall asleep.

There's a house down by the docks on Eik Island, a rather old wooden house, with a dark door and that faded sign of the postal horn on the wall. There's a man sitting in there, the old postmaster Karl Magnus Skogmann, and the school teacher on the island, Henrietta Brunberg.

He wants her to enjoy sitting there with him, because he realizes how good it is for him to have her there. He tries to keep his comments to a minimum so that what he does say will carry weight, but soon forgets himself altogether and can talk freely, and hears her saying to him:

"Maybe it is just as well to resign oneself to the fact that things don't turn out the way one had expected. It isn't the end even if you have to give up all your demands. I mean, when I fight for my rights I make *him* feel bad. But when I don't, I become *bad* myself, full of pent up meanness.

"When our daughter leaves one day, will I stay here for his sake? He might get along better without me. It's just that I don't dare to make the break myself; I wouldn't be able to straighten out my life any better without him.

"I guess what I am really saying is that it's me there's something wrong with; I can't cope because I am greedy, dissatisfied, inconsiderate, mean. And to combat all this, it feels like everything healthy in me is rising up in a scream of protest: No! But I've been brought up to turn anything bad that happens against myself, because I don't have any decent explanation for it otherwise. I'm a bad person, so I can't do anything good. And yet I know that's not true. I want to be good, but that door is closed for me now, and I just don't see any way out, none at all."

She holds her head in her hands and he sits and looks at her peeking out through her fingers: "Do you understand me? Do you understand what I am saying to you, Skogmann?" And he answers:

"I don't know."

He looks at the clock; it's after twelve. He asks: "It doesn't look like Brunberg is going to come and get you . . ."

"No, he most likely won't. Can I stay a while longer?"

"You can stay as long as you like."

"Because he isn't coming to get me. That's why I want to stay a while longer."

"I understand that," says Skogmann. "Because you've started a war now, haven't you? It was a choice you made, and I, old man that I am and in favor of peace and reconciliation my whole life, can't be your advisor in war,"

there is a man writing in Oslo; he turns off the rain before the teacher Henrietta Brunberg is to go home, but lets squalls pass by Skogmann's house, hurls them past the docks on Eik Island, until three in the morning, and Henrietta gets up and says: "Thanks very much, Skogmann."

he gets up and goes with her out onto the road, she doesn't want to let him be a gentleman and walk her home. He sees in the gale that this grand specimen of womanhood is little and thin and says: "Your suitcases will stay here. For the time being."

She walks in the wet wind, and thinks it feels good, but is ashamed of all the things she has told the old man. But there isn't anyone else here! No one! And defends herself: Will it have to get so bad that I start screaming before I find a natural occasion to talk this out with someone,

on arrival there are lights in all the windows, she is nearly blinded as she stands in the doorway and looks into the smoke-filled room where Arve is sitting, alone, stiff; he barely manages to raise his eyes when she comes in,

"You didn't come to get me," she says, attempting to say it casually,

"and since you have to go to work tomorrow, you should have gone to bed long ago!"

He keeps staring,

"Don't you understand," he says quietly, "that I am calling your name?"

9

For the man writing this, the evening remains out there in darkness. He leans over his typewriter and thinks he is leaning over the railing of a boat, and feels the lead sinker on his fishing gear hit bottom a long way down there. He feels the line go limp in his hand, hauls the evening in and puts it in a well in the bottom of the boat, stays hunched over untangling the knots all night long, all the way till dawn comes and he realizes: I have to go there. He takes his suitcase down from the closet and a taxi to Fornebu Airport. The plane to Molde is on the runway, but is delayed on account of the cloud cover, and he sits in the waiting area while

Marianna Kretsen from Eik Island wakes up in her room, in a basement on Langfot Road in Ramvik, wakes up and sees that Hans has really overslept. A small gray stripe between the curtains tells her that it must be past seven o'clock. With his back to her on the narrow divan the guy named Hans lies sleeping.

"Hans! It's after seven!"

Marianna is out of bed, turns on the burner, and goes to the bathroom down the hall.

After seven. In a few seconds he's into his pants and calls to her: "If I'm not there on the dot, he'll fire me this time!"

"Can a few minutes make any difference? Don't you want to wait until I make some coffee?" But the instant she says "coffee" she runs back out to the toilet again and pukes.

On her return she sees that he is hurrying into his overcoat, has pulled back the curtains and cracked open the window a bit. Against the morning light that filters in steadily, she can clearly see how young he is, facial features that aren't marked by anything at all, that wrinkle in his forehead was just stuck on there this morning, he is narrow in the shoulders, and despite his coal black hair has no shadow on his cheek to give a hint of beard. He was well prepared and seemed confident when he came the evening before; now he has nothing to hide behind, she looks at him and is slightly amazed.

"What is it?" he asks.

"Come by the cafe when you're on your break, would you?"

"If I can." Then: "Don't worry, we'll manage."

"It'll work out."

"You'll surely find someone who can get rid of it, and then the whole thing will be forgotten," he says. But wishes right away he hadn't said it. She has walked him to the door and backs away when he says that last phrase, tries to kiss him anyway, feels that sleep has settled in her lips, they are numb like her brain, but the light is unrelenting and calls for more serious reflection. She goes to the disheveled divan to sleep a little more, she doesn't have to get up yet, but turns on the radio so she doesn't go out completely. The music congregates around a bright spot far inside her; she falls asleep or dozes again, and dreams that the warm bed is a man she can cling to, but one who makes her feel nauseous and need to throw up;

she remains hanging like that between sleep and drowsiness. In the room beyond the covers: the frost she is trying to withdraw from, the taste in her mouth which is dry, the stiff, crusty eyelids. The numbers on the alarm clock light up a full 24 hours. Her brain is working with a film and whirls around, whirls around. Half asleep she can operate, but not stop the machine; she is lying on a divan in a basement room, feeling a crowd of people going in and out of her body. She sees Hans standing a long time with his back to her. He is fooling with the wires on a record player, holding a screwdriver in his hands like when she saw him for the first time, twisting two wire ends together with his thumbs, hard; she notices that he has beautiful hands. She always looks to see if men have beautiful hands, but isn't sure whether or not she has gotten this from a book about a young woman she liked so well,

it happened in summer, this scene that now glides slowly past, and she changes it a bit so that it will be beautiful and believable. She and Metta have just begun to work at the Bus Station Cafe, they have passed by the company office on the first floor, where Metta complained about her wages until she forced them up fifty crowns a month, and they came into the glowing hot kitchen, where she said: "It's a good thing we won't have to work in here at least!" But it would be quite warm in the cafe area too,

then she and Metta climb out through the window of the cafe and over to the roof of the kitchen which is a bit lower—they are out for a break and some fresh air and there is a light breeze blowing out there. They see a young man climbing up the wall of the Big Cross, the new city hall which will soon be finished, they sit and talk about everything and nothing; the guy climbing there is apparently going to attach a rope to the roof (or whatever). Metta calls over to him: "Watch out that you don't fall!" He climbs higher and higher on the metal ladder propped close up to the wall (there's a guy down there holding it), higher and higher, until he is all the way up, waves to them, flings himself over onto the roof,

and then?

Well, then he comes into the cafe an hour later and orders a cup of coffee, and Metta says they don't serve just coffee, he'll have to order some food, just to be difficult. After that they get acquainted with him and he comes again. Secretly they fight over him behind the counter, over which of them will take him his order, but the one who loses can always go over and empty his ashtray afterwards. (If there isn't a lot to do.) Then the guy shows up later one evening at Metta's place; stands there with his back turned fixing the wires on the record player, and then we play some records when he is done. Afterwards we go out, just hang around outside because it is so darned light at night that sleeping is out of the question and because we both have the afternoon shift. He has to go to work early the next day, but it doesn't matter. He doesn't need any sleep now, he says. Wondering why he's out walking with us and not saying anything about there being two of us. We sit on the edge of the road, talking nonsense and looking over at Eik Island, and I say that I never want to go back there, and he takes my hand. We can pretend that's what he does, but Metta tries to come between us because she doesn't want anything like that getting started and begins to talk politics with him; I think it's sort of embarrassing. But she gives up, glides out of the picture, there was that student who was around here, but often when I'm on the afternoon shift I wonder if maybe she's meeting Hans without my knowing about it,

when you get right down to it, it *isn't* Hans I'm thinking about, it must be another guy, but he looks just the same anyway,

but when the alarm clock rings neither one of them is there, and she gets scared immediately, thinking that she is alone with a child, can't get to work and if she can't get to work, what will she live on, and she won't get to go out a single evening any more either, will she? But it isn't her fault if it turns out like that; suddenly she realizes this, and she fumbles in the closet looking for that damned peasant costume she took home to wash, the innocent white blouse with its silly peacock frills, the dirndl skirt she has hemmed up to suit her. It isn't raining outside, but the anorak is still damp when she puts it on. When she hurries out into the street after having splashed a little water on her face and run a comb through her hair which looks disheveled because she got so wet yesterday, she sees the Eik Island ferry coming, out in the fjord, and she knows that her father is standing at the front of the car deck with his brown briefcase under his arm,

and the man writing this calculates a ticket price for the twenty minutes the crossing takes; it runs from Ramvik to Vind Island and from Vind Island to Land Island and from Land Island to Eik Island and from Eik Island back to Ramvik, all day long, with the ferry crew split into two shifts, like the two shifts at the cafe. He figures out what the price on a cup of coffee would be if you were to include the value-added tax. He watches as the kitchen staff carries in fresh baked goods from the bus from town, and hurries to fill up the glass case before the customers come. And then maybe he'll have to write a letter to the county tax assessor in Molde about the hard times for business; what will people do with themselves if the cafe is shut down when they arrive on the ferry or are about to leave on the bus? Sit in the waiting room? where the walls are full of hearts and names,

10

when Karl Magnus Skogmann, the former postmaster on Eik Island gets up early, in his house, which he keeps in order, and walks on the feet of an old man to the electric range and turns on the burner, before he lets the shades up and looks out at the weather on the fjord,

he glimpses the name Christopher Bruun on the photograph hanging on the wall. The hands on the clock say it's eight, it is gray and windy, but the sky is bright with big clouds racing over Eik Island Sound. In his own and Bruun's democratic thoughts he thinks how the day will turn out *in this poor land, edged with sloping rock*, the old sentences run through his head like peas. He feels for the first time in a long time that he is old, he doesn't dwell on what happened the evening before, but it is firmly wedged in his body. *Freedom* and *Will* have been forgotten in European philosophy for the benefit of *a rigid necessity, prescribed by law*, he pours down a cup of coffee and feels he has to get started on something or other. He casts a sidelong glance at his stamp-collecting album lying open on a table, but that is all in order; he thinks about the books behind the glass doors in the cabinet, they have all been pretty well scrutinized. And the house is just the way it should be; he has to go out.

Here we can scarcely speak of socialism; we also have a relatively great degree of charity, which counteracts coldness and hatred

here on Eik Island before the snow comes, he plants his hat on his head and puts on his cape, goes in to get his wallet which is lying in a drawer and begins to amble down the road. The wind is at the back of this blithe man stepping carefully to avoid the rain puddles, and he floats along barely touching the ground. He thinks to himself—if I didn't know how to walk the right way, I guess I'd blow right out to sea...

He strides off the road at Old Anna's house; the sky is shining up from puddles all around, the sheep are shaking the water off themselves over by the mountain wall, and he supports himself on the wind like a large bird, while he waits for it to get late enough that he won't have to make any comment on the morning's radio devotions when he goes into the house.

He is offered a chair when he comes in and says: "I would like to see if there are any more books in the book collection that I haven't read."

"There is so much garbage and godlessness that I am ashamed to lend them out." The quaking old woman sits in the chair by the stove, knitting. "I ought to tell them I don't want to be in charge of the People's Library!" But at least the books are being lent out...

He goes into a little room next to her bedroom where the crates of books in the Eik Island People's Library line the walls. They come on the ferry across the fjord from Ramvik and are replaced with a new batch a couple of times a year. He opens the various crates, but finds he has already read most of the books. In the philosophy corner he stops at a volume called *Perspectives in Social Democracy*, pulls out the card catalogue drawer and makes note, as usual, of which book he is borrowing in painstakingly neat block letters, and the signature—Karl Magnus Skogmann—with a large flourish,

back in the kitchen, coffee is waiting for him. He sits down and digs with one fingernail in his tobacco tin while saying: "I got to thinking about your husband Andreas as I walked up the hills here; he'd have been 70 years old today, if he were still alive,"

and he could tell by looking at the old woman that it hit her hard that she hadn't remembered the date; she started talking nervously about her husband; nobody had been like him; who would have believed he would pass on so long before his time? He was like a thirty-year-old when they buried him; he didn't look a day over thirty, no sir, not a single day, but you don't think that's because he took life easy, do you? No sir, he was busy as could be from morning to night! And you think he ever said a harsh word to me? No sir, never, and he looked like a youngster to the day he died, and Karl Magnus Skogmann pictured *the full might of manhood* in Christopher Bruun, then pictured a man who sat down by the docks mending nets the final years of his life, a shriveled and shrunken hulk of a human being, hunched over and disfigured by the disease you weren't allowed to mention by name, sat like a shadow by the boathouse wall, mending nets, while the white spring sunlight came cascading across the sound and swirled around him,

so that the man writing has to pull the shades down in the teacher's house further up on the island and go around emptying ashtrays and cleaning up for Arve Brunberg who is still sitting in his chair, smoking cigarettes late at night, after Henrietta has come home. Towards morning he notices that it has stopped raining; he walks out in the darkness to let the wind blow on him. Henrietta has gone into the guestroom and is asleep there. But she didn't lock the door behind her. Was this her way of saying that he was allowed to go in there? he peeks in the door several times, but she doesn't move; he has to go back and sit in the living room again and swallow his great defeat. At first he thinks he won't go to work the next day, but the thought of what they might say to each other when she woke up makes him decide to go anyway. He has to leave before seven, shaves and munches on a piece of bread. There is still plenty of time. He tiptoes up to look in at her once more. The ceiling light is on above the bed; Henrietta is lying on top of the covers, sleeping soundly; the dress, shoes and stockings she stripped off are lying in a heap on the floor. The room has an aroma of perfume, a kind he has never smelled before, and there she lies, a thousand miles away from him in her sleep; he can stare at her all he wants; she is gone; he cannot get to her. "Two nights out carousing, it's no wonder you're sleeping," he thinks bitterly, and suddenly feels like beating her awake, forcing her to wake up, pulling her up by the hair, pounding it into her that he cares about her. But she just lies there. He knew that if he were considering killing her she would go to bed like that all the same, because he would never have the courage to do it. He looks around; he begins to hear singing inside his head, like the humming sound from transformers and electric power plants; he sees a pair of scissors lying on the bathroom counter; he goes and gets them, bends over her and pulls up her bra a little bit so that he can get the scissors under the elastic between the cups, snips it open, and pulls it off her. Snips her sheer panties open at both hips; she moans faintly as if she were about to wake up, but she doesn't. He stands there looking at her as one looks at a corpse just before they haul it away, then finally covers her up and leaves the room, goes out to the road, and jogs down toward the docks to make the ferry to Ramvik,

and the man writing this lets the ferry chug out to sea, impossible to cancel it, and he convinces Arve Brunberg that it will be easier to face the day if he gets enough fresh air. He lets the man stand bracing himself against the railing at the front of the car deck, and sends the ticket seller up to collect the three crowns he feels it's only reasonable to charge for this trip; he has the ticket seller shout into Brunberg's ear: "It's too late to look at the scenery now!"

"We office rats need all the fresh air we can get! As for the landscape, it's never been much to look at . . ." Just then Olver Kretsen comes up from the salon and stands there, swaying and staring over toward Ramvik clutching his brown satchel and a pair of mittens Anna-Marja forced him to take along; they usually exchange a few inconsequential remarks, but this particular day it's not easy to talk about the weather; it's lucky the wind gives them a good excuse for not chatting on this crossing, these fellows on deck, people on the move, men of responsibility who sight land on the other side of Eik Island Sound in the age-old way with their feet spaced wide, Arve Brunberg off to his job to show that he is somebody, Olver Kretsen, to feed his family, and the ferry approaching shore, one passenger after another emerging from the salon; they note the busses to Molde parked by the Bus Station Cafe, waiting, the sign on the wall at the ferry dock about not riding bicycles on the wharves, the clattering of a truck motor left idling; they both have to wait a quarter of an hour in the Bus Station Cafe,

11

where Marianna Kretsen unlocks the door from the inside for two bus drivers who come to order their morning coffee at the counter. They have driven their busses from Molde. One of them says:

"Did you notice that the boat out at Eik Island's gone?"

"The weather must have gotten too tough for the researchers."

They go over to a table; maybe one of them is holding a copy of "The Romsdal Messenger" in his hand, and studies the wire-service articles about a Swedish pop group, which started out as three normal guys who played at dances in the area around Vasterås, but managed to get out of doing that pretty fast. One of the drivers reports a dream he had in the night and just remembered when he saw the newspaper: it was the Phantom from the comic strips, the one who has been alive for 400 years and been locked up in the publishing office all that time. One day he breaks out through the brick wall and gets out onto Storgata in Molde. He goes into that innocent little paint store called Jørgen Gjenstad, you know the one, and buys 400 liters of red paint and paints the whole town red, the streets and everything, so that the busses driving inland along Frænavegen and out across Julsundet leave red stripes behind their wheels. Marianna Kretsen stands behind the counter, listening; he shouts to her:

"Marianna, come over here!"

and he asks her if she is going to the dance at the Ramvik Hotel that evening. The other fellow feels around for his keys, getting ready to start his return trip.

"You may as well cancel your run," says Marianna. "Nobody from Eik Island is going to Molde today anyway. They only go to town when there's a sale going on. The ones who work in Molde drive themselves."

"I better get going now. Did you notice those two poor fools I drove over from Molde this morning?"

"Who were they?"

"The mayor came and met them at the bus."

"Oh, so they were that sort."

The door drifted slowly shut behind him.

But Marianna asks the fellow still sitting there, hunched over his newspaper, if he meant what he said about the dance, if it was actually his intention to invite her, and he looks at her amazed. She disappears to get a tray of fresh open-face sandwiches to put in the glass case. He yells after her:

"Yes, but I thought you preferred to stick with sons of directors and things . . ."

"Oh, so you think I'm stuck up?"

"Is it all over between you and Hans now?"

"Could be."

"We could reserve a table," he says. It is so rare that anything happens in those parts.

"That's fine, if Metta can come and meet us there when she gets off work tonight."

"She can do that, but she'll have to find her own date."

"I'm sure she can manage that."

Through the door into the cafe walks Olver Kretsen, a man between fifty and sixty, a formerly powerful man, along with the fellow from the Welfare Office. He goes over to the window and sits down there, just like he always does. So he can look out at the fjord. Then Marianna comes over with coffee for him. If it's her shift. As a rule there are not many people at this time of day, so she can chat with him. He might say: "Well, here you are again," and she would say: "Yes, here I am." Today he says: "How are things going with you?" despite the fact that Brunberg is there, and Marianna answers: "Fine, thanks. And with you?" He looks at her, confused; she's pulling something new on him. He is forced to answer: "With me? Things are going like usual, I guess." "Yes, I guess they are," says Marianna.

Brunberg says: "I'd like some coffee myself." He rubs his cold hands together and looks out at the fjord like Olver. Marianna is over at the glass counter, filling his cup. With her back to them she works feverishly to gain control of her expression: No one is supposed to have an inkling, no one. She is a picture, a familiar face from a magazine, a young girl making coffee for her father and a neighbor, while they are in the midst of an important conversation. She forces back nausea by thinking over and over again: "It's only coffee, for God's sake!" and balances it on a tray over to the table with the sugar cubes in her apron pocket. She puts it down and tosses the cubes onto the table, one by one. Arve Brunberg says cockily: "Well, well, well. How's it going?" and stirs his coffee. But he can't fool anyone with that face of his. She bends down and whispers to him, loudly: "Did you get drunk yesterday, Brunberg? You look so blurry-eyed today." Her father gives a start in his chair and gets a dark look on his face: "What on earth do you think you're doing, asking our neighbor a question like that?" But Brunberg just roars with laughter: "Ha, ha, ha, yes, I guess you might call it drunk!" Then he slumps over, stares out, silence everywhere, and Marianna hurries back to the counter.

When they look up and out the window they notice it, both of them—the boat out by Eik Island has disappeared, and without wanting to, they look at each other. Olver: "Yes, they must be gone now, those researchers." He reaches for his cap, getting ready to leave, nods at Marianna, says to Brunberg that "your wife must be off today, since the children have autumn vacation," and Brunberg looks at him suspiciously, ready to leave also: "What about it?" and Olver answers that as far as having time off goes, they have it pretty easy, the teachers, that is, but then they need it, since the kids are so difficult. "Are they?" asks Brunberg and Olver answers that he doesn't know, he's just heard that's the case . . . More people come in as they walk out, on their way over to the Big Cross, where Arve Brunberg will head upstairs and Olver Kretsen down to the basement. Help the janitor keep everything in good order. They are standing on the wet asphalt between the buildings, surrounded by the bustle of people hurrying to work.

"Can you come over to my place this evening, Kretsen? There's something I want to talk to you about."

"There isn't anything wrong, is there?"

"It's about that boat that has been anchored out by the island. Do you think it's research they're doing?"

"I don't know anything about it. But if there is something you can explain to me . . ."

"Things are not the way they should be, Kretsen."

12

He has tossed out an island, beyond the borders of civilization, a little windswept society on the west coast of Norway, a splotch on the ocean, a growth in a remote area. It has been several years since it made any sense to go out for the winter herring catch, but people manage to get out of their beds each morning all the same; they tear the pages off the calendar and let a new day take the place of the old one. In dark metal boxes all around, the electricity meters are ticking; there is no danger mentioned in the paper, for the water is rising in the storage tanks at the Aura Power Company, even though winter is approaching. The man writing is dangling by a thread in mid-air on a regular Braathen flight from Oslo, and Molde's Årø Airport, scheduled for completion the following year, is suddenly all finished, just for him. He takes a taxi to Romsdalheimen Hotel, but can't give the desk clerk an answer about how long he'll be staying. On the way up to his room with his suitcase he sees a map of Romsdal County, checks out the area he is interested in and mumbles: "The same old nonsense." Since he can't settle down with his theories over a cup of coffee in the dining room, he makes his way along Storgata in the drizzle to the bus depot where he gets a bus to a cafe up in the mountain pass, a cafe where he can sit and get an overview. In October. And then, once he's up there, he sees nothing but fog and more fog; heavyhearted, he has to lay his notebook on the table: he has come here to get close to his characters, can't see them clearly, but they do exist! he thinks stubbornly, and starts fooling around, trying to make Anna-Marja Kretsen visible in his notebook, where she

is standing by the window after Olver has disappeared out the door in the morning and taken his bike to get down to the ferry in time. Anna-Marja looks at the clock—he could have made it without the bicycle. The youngest of the boys, who is eight, munches on a bread crust at the table, pulls a knitted cap down over his ears and dashes out. She removes the dishes from the table; the work goes faster when no one is watching. The teacher's husband runs past out on the road; he, too, wants to make the ferry; they all have plenty of time. She takes the potato peelings and the remains of yesterday's dinner out to the outbuilding where ten or fifteen chickens come flapping down from their roosting places and begin eating greedily; she puts her hand into one of the nesting boxes and pulls it back out with three slightly warm eggs. She comes back into the house, finds that the twelve-year-old boy has gotten up. He has cut his own slices of bread, stuffs them down while thumbing through a comic book his father has bought for him, then gets dressed and runs out. She calls after him, he answers that he's going up and see if that big boat is still moored there, and she says, "Don't go down to the water today!" And then she's alone,

and she pours herself some lukewarm coffee from the pot on the stove and sits down with the newspaper, *The Romsdal Messenger*, 75 øre, vol. 128. As long as Olver is in the house she can never relax enough to sit down. In the kitchen cabinet, behind the sacks with sugar and flour there is a bottle of pills; she takes one; he doesn't even know she has them. Afterwards she sucks a sugar cube in the side of her mouth and lets her eyes glide up and down the newspaper columns. Anything for her? Weddings and births and funerals? Doesn't interest her. But she combs the want ads ever so carefully because she would really like to know if there is any job in the world that she might be fit for. She doesn't take it seriously, perhaps, but she just wants to check and see. Because now that the children are bigger she has often said to Olver that she would like to have a job, since she doesn't know what to do with herself all day, and he says,

"It might be difficult to find something here on the island,"

and this meant it was out of the question, for someone had to be there to greet the kids when they came home from school, and she knew that he thought no one would give her a job even if there were one to be had; he thought she was so slow that she could just barely manage to keep the house in order. "But I am *becoming* slow, because I have to stretch what little housework there is so that it lasts to the end of the day."

Finally it happened that she got hired to wash some floors over at the school where nobody asked how fast she did it because she worked for a fixed wage. She manages to finish before Olver comes home from work if she goes over there just when the school day is over so that she meets the school children coming out the gate. The sixty crowns a week she earns she puts in with the egg money in a jar and calls it her own. Once a month she asks Olver, "What shall we do with this money?" He answers that she may do whatever she likes, "After all, it's your money." But she wants to know if he has any ideas about what she might buy with it. "Buy something for yourself," he says then, "some clothes you can wear when we go . . ." But she interrupts, "What do I need new clothes for? We never go any place anyway." But he would gladly go visiting people quite often; it's just that she doesn't want to, he claims. And she says, of course she doesn't want to, because she doesn't have anything to wear,

so she had better correct that by making a trip to Ramvik the next day; he begs her to do it. She wants to take the twelve-o'clock ferry over, barely manages to make herself presentable so that she dares to be seen on the boat and in the places she has to go into in Ramvik, but she walks slowly past the display windows with women's wear and wanders over toward the post office which has moved to the Big Cross. For way down in the bottom of her black purse she always has an electricity bill she has to pay and she gets in the line that forms every morning and waits holding the hundred-crown notes and coins she has sorted out from the cake tin and put into her coin purse. It doesn't take much time at all to get rid of money; the rubber stamp of the Post Office Bank slams down on the receipt and the money disappears through the little window. For Marianna's sake she almost never goes to the Bus Station Cafe like other people when they go over to Ramvik to shop, but once in a while she takes the elevator up to the doctor's office, petrified of meeting someone from the island there, which happens now and then. She has to have an explanation ready to give in case they are sitting there and look up from the weekly magazines that are laid out in the waiting room when she comes in the door.

"Your back still giving you problems, Anna-Marja?"

"It sure is. I should have gone to town and gotten treatment, but I never get around to it, and the public health insurance doesn't cover it either."

"It's probably sciatica."

"The doctor isn't quite sure what it is."

But inside the office the doctor says to her, "Can't we get along just as well without those pills, Mrs. Kretsen? It's such a small dose you're taking."

"It's nice to have them around, just in case."

THE FERRY CROSSING

And he says that's probably a good idea, and as long as she sticks to this level of use there's no danger. He bends over and makes some additional markings on the wrinkled prescription which she takes along to the pharmacy afterwards. And now here she sits. With her elbows on the plastic table cloth, both hands around her coffee cup, and the newspaper on the table with the want ads facing up. Doesn't expect to find anything really, probably wouldn't apply even if she found something right down her narrow alley, just wants to see what sort of people they're looking for. If nobody is offering her a job, it must mean nobody needs her either, nobody. It's easy to think that way. But she has the children, doesn't she? Impatient as they are to get out from under her wings, manage on their own. When her fingers are just itching to help the little one put his clothes on, he howls: "Go away! I want to do it myself!" And he is growing right along, his shoes keep getting too small, pants too short, and she is proud because he can manage on his own and is moving in wider and wider circles away from her, yet meanwhile she knows that the day he takes the ferry across Eik Island Sound it will be all over. For her, anyway, knowing that she'll have no purpose in life when she doesn't have them at home anymore; her arms get numb all the way up to her elbows when she thinks about Marianna. Something or other is going on with that girl. But wasn't she herself just sitting here now . . . like this! If she had something to take the place of them when they were gone, she wouldn't have had any reason to get so worried about Marianna.

Whew, she sighs, but can't quite relax,

sees Skogmann standing out on the road staring at something or other; she pushes herself to get moving, gets up and walks around in case he should happen to look in the window and see her. She could just as well talk to him, she's known him a long time and has nothing to be afraid of, but can't go out and call to him because she's alone in the house. It's not her he's coming to see. "He doesn't think I'm worth talking to. He talks to everyone, but if he talks to me it's just because he thinks I need it," and sure enough, just as she thought, he is not going to her place. He turns on his heels and heads straight across the road to Krok-Anna's house.

Anna-Marja Kretsen has gone up to the second floor to straighten up the beds when the twelve-year-old comes clomping in high-top boots across the kitchen floor beneath her and all out of breath yells from the stairs: "Two men are coming down on the road. I think they're coming here!" She casts one glance out the window and another down at her clothes, that flowered apron she's wearing; she can't let people see her like this. Her head is a muddle: "What shall I put on? what shall I put on?" She walks around in circles, opens closet doors, digs around, garments fall down, she throws them on the bed, runs over to a mirror to look at her hair, can't let anyone see her this way! Shoves the boy toward the stairs, whispers: "Go! Go down and say I'll be there soon." And what if they can tell that she has taken that little pill?

13

. . .while the man writing takes up the question of Marianna's pregnancy, clips out her silhouette, just as Hans Kristiansson asks her that evening before they fall asleep: "When did you go to the doctor, Marianna?" "A couple of days ago. I called from home . . ."

now Hans' bicycle has been stolen and he is running down Langfot Road from Marianna's flat. Some practical joker or other just can't keep his hands off other people's bikes. Drives around in a truck and picks up bicycles that are lying along the edge of the road, sells them and makes money on it. But what the hell am I supposed to do now; this is no time to get into trouble at work. He runs. Past the Big Cross, the Bus Station Cafe, past the businesses in the center of Ramvik, out along the highway, up a hill. They've got too much on me already, damn it! damn it! Now I'm really screwing myself. He comes to a construction site on a plateau with the sign "Happiness Heights." Right on, man, the height of happiness, and the names of the contractor and the sub-contractor and the electrician and the interior decorator crap and the son-of-a-bitch architect. He knows where he's headed and walks the final stretch to catch his breath. A couple of minutes one way or the other, Marianna had said. But he never gets there. The engineer is just coming out of the construction barracks: "Kristiansson, come here! How long do you think we can put up with this?" He says he's sorry, it won't happen again. "We've heard that before, time and time again." "Let me explain..." "I don't give a damn about your explanations. You are a hell of a lot more trouble than you're worth around here." "But I'm an innocent victim..." "We called your place and you didn't come home last night." "Well, but what the hell..." "I promised your father to give you a chance!" "Don't bring him into this!" "I've called and told him." "Come on, man, hell, I've got big problems." "They don't concern us. You damn loafer! You are impossible. Showing up here like this with your record. You are useless. Look, we decide to give you a chance, pretend not to notice when you screw around, defend you against landladies and... and get you a new place to live, and get you this and get you that... You know what you ought to do? You ought to pack your bags. Volunteer for Vietnam! Go to hell! And no backtalk! The rest of your wages will be mailed. If you have any coming, that is. Goodbye!"

He sees them turn around—the guys he used to work with—and grin mockingly. He grins back, but his jaw goes stiff when he sees that not one of them will come to his aid, they all think he's an idiot. He turns his back and walks toward the road. Back to Marianna? Back to Marianna and complain about his rotten treatment? No. Better get myself to Molde. Try to talk some sense into Dad. It's only a matter of money. What difference does it make. What's the point of going to Ramvik and trying to get your life squared away? You'll just find out it won't work. Better promise the old man something or other. I'm all he's got. Tell him I'll take the college entrance exams, or whatever. I've gotta have money. Get rid of that embryo. That's impossible here in Ramvik. To get an abortion here the mother would have to be a cripple and the father mentally retarded. There was an address in Oslo, who told me about that place? Shit, why can't I remember? There's a bus leaving soon. No time to figure this out. There's the bus stop, just jump on. He sees the bus coming around the bend, runs to catch it. The bus almost runs into him, but it's just a practical joke, of course, he knows the driver, who's sitting there grinning. He sits down up at the front and starts looking for his wallet. But he hasn't got it and it wouldn't make any difference if he did, he had to count out his last øre for beer yesterday. He leans over to the driver: "Fredrik! I forgot my wallet." "Then I'll have to kick you off at the next stop." "Get serious. You'll get the money when I come back this afternoon." "You want me to believe that?" But he's allowed to stay on, no sweat. Fredrik drives fast and jerkily. Hans sits thinking about Marianna.

At first she was so closed up. No wonder he was so dead set on getting through to her. But once he was there, the sky was the limit. They had a great time. Things were fine. But the trouble with Marianna is that she's not terribly exciting once you get used to her. She just doesn't have any, uh, . . . imagination. Yeah, that's it. She has no imagination. She's too serious. That's the problem. And he grasps the aluminum railing next to the seat as the bus jerks along, because it's the only thing he's got to hang on to.

14

Metta Nilsen is a different case. Take Metta Nilsen, for instance—she is always in control. She gets up in the morning and rubs cold water on her face and checks in the mirror to see if everything is how it should be. But she has no business being up this early, what's she going to do before her shift starts at 3:30, besides hang around this room of hers? But no,

she puts on her fine, red coat, the one with the special resistance to the dust and dirt in the streets of Ramvik, and takes it off again to put on matching make-up. Puts it back on. And red shoes! And a red purse! She had all this with her when she came back home two years ago, after a quick stint at sea and went ashore in Bergen where she changed clothes in the restroom of a cafe and stuffed her old shoes and her old coat beneath the lid of a bulging suitcase.

Then she takes the train home. Past the small stations along the Bergen line up to Myrdal, gets off at the windswept mountain station and goes into the cafe there. Waiting for the cog train that glides down into Flåm Valley, the place where she lives, or used to live, where she'll sit in a corner of the living room and catch up on the time she has been away from them: her father, her mother, her brothers and sisters standing at attention while she takes off the red coat and places the purse next to her chair. All of them thinking the same thought about the foreign smell of perfume she has brought home with her. Can they read in her face the things she has experienced while away? She digs in her purse to find a magazine and all the brothers and sisters gather around to look: what kind of a magazine is that? One about her coat, it would seem.

Unexpectedly, she is accepted at the Folk High School where Marianna Kretsen goes. Metta is so much older than the others that it bothers her in the beginning. Later on she doesn't think so much about it. She is not exactly sure what happened to her that winter, but if someone were to ask, she might say that she had discovered herself, and they would have stood there wondering if that was all there was to it. But for her it comes down to this: not feeling like you're floating aimlessly. She reads books to find out who she is, they come close to describing her, and she turns to Marianna to talk one evening. Marianna.

That little timid being from Eik Island way up on the coast somewhere, as shy of people as you can get, what can we do with Marianna? Metta knows. And she does it. Unties one knot after another and when she happens to spot Marianna kissing a boy around the corner of the boarding school one evening, she considers her job finished, and she thinks it's time to focus on other things. But somehow or other she slips into a friendship with Marianna. They become very close and the whole school notices it and calls them Marimetta, but who cares? They laugh for a whole evening after Marianna says, "It is so wholesome around this place that I can't stand it!" And they support each other in their careful opposition to the polished surface and the friendly tone that even the youngest teachers are afflicted with when they have taught there for a while, the sticky sweet voices they use when they want to fool you into ideals that are two sizes too large and cause you to trip and fall on your nose. Then along comes spring and they are supposed to group themselves on the school steps and sing or whatever, the earth is alive, white table cloths and budding youth around the table, the total absence of tobacco smoke and nicotine-yellow fingers and everything that breaks the body down, complete harmony all day long, which only a few of them can continue to believe in: the ones who find each other beneath the blue spring skies or are sent there by parents with lots of books on their shelves. The ones who seem to be cemented into their national costumes at graduation and manage to cherish their youthful ideals without getting their feet muddy after school, but rather read modern poetry and have their children when they can afford it. And then they buy themselves records with music from the Folk High School and chamber music and romances. Marianna and Metta are not in this group. They do their homework, but they can't handle the essays in style. They become absorbed by another form of intellectuality which may be cut from the same cloth, but which nevertheless distinguishes them from the rest: they wear long pants and denim jeans and drag their chairs out into the drafty outer hall where smoking is permitted and discuss the books they have read: A *Doctor's Guide*. It is about the human body and they discover that they now have a language to discuss it in,

and later on they arrive in Molde and get on the bus for the ride to Ramvik on a warm, dusty day in summer, looking for a job while they think about what to do with their lives. The grand transformation they are waiting for does not take place. They find out that they can be there until Christmas in any event, and can use the time to look for work in Oslo. That's where they want to go, of course. Metta is becoming vaguely aware that time is running short and she has to find something to do, anything

but she is still here. It is the 30th of October. The white wind blows in from the west and the gravel road she walks on in her red shoes after coming down the stairs is wet and rutted. But the sky has cleared off for the moment, as if someone had gone over it with a dustcloth. She catches the bus and gets off in front of the Bus Station Cafe, where the children are pouring out the door, the mothers hurrying across the square toward the shops on the other side, toward the pharmacy, the post office and the Bus Station Cafe, where they have a cup of coffee and gather energy before or after their round of shopping. Metta comes into the Big Cross and asks where the office of the Social Services Counselor is and if she may speak with him. The elevator takes her up to the sixth floor, she walks down the corridor to a door with a number on it, an office where she takes a seat in the outer room and waits.

A well-dressed man in his thirties placed behind the polished surface of a desk in there; a nice guy who looks at Metta Nilsen in a friendly way when she comes in the door. Just look at all the big ring binders on the shelf behind him, and the reference books and debate proceedings he reads, and a map of greater Ramvik including the three islands. He smiles at Metta Nilsen and she doesn't exactly look ready to snap his head off. I surely don't look like I'd bite anyone, now do I? He sits scrutinizing the red outfit she has put on for the occasion, and he says: "Yes?" and she places her purse on her lap.

"It's about a request for an abortion."

He gets up and introduces himself: "Halvor Børresen."

Then he says: "It's been warm in Ramvik this summer."

"What is that supposed to mean?"

"Oh, just that you're not the first to make such a request. That doctor isn't in favor of it and he passes you all along to me!"

She shakes her head when he offers her a cigarette and takes her own out of her bag. He lights it for her

"You may not be 100 percent sure that you don't want this baby, you know. I mean, this is a difficult business you're getting involved in now."

"But it's not me!"

"What did you say?"

"I'm here on behalf of a girlfriend."

"It's one of your girlfriends who is pregnant?"

"Right."

"But why didn't she come herself?"

"She's at work today, and tomorrow you're probably closed here since it's Saturday."

"Yes."

"And we really wanted to get going on this before the weekend."

"But you realize that she will have to come up here herself, don't you?"

"I want to make an appointment for her, so she can come up this afternoon."

"Of course. Does she know that you are here now?"

"No, not exactly. But she doesn't know what else she can do other than come here to find a doctor who will do it, and she is afraid to come here."

"Why?"

"Because there are a lot of people in the building who know her. Her father works here and we don't want anyone to know about this."

"She doesn't want to have the baby?"

"She can't have the baby."

"But what about the father?"

"The father?"

"Yes, the baby's father!"

"It's all over with him."

"But what does he want?"

"Does that have anything to do with this? Like I said, it's over."

"But maybe they'll solve their problems, now that this has happened."

"Do you think this would be a 'solution'"?

"I don't know. But I do know that you have to have compelling reasons at this place."

"Isn't it a compelling enough reason that she is not *able* to take care of the baby herself?"

"I'm not the one who makes the decisions in these cases."

"No, I know that."

"I would say that her chances are slim if there is nothing wrong with her. But she had better come herself."

"Can I make an appointment for her?"

"I'll keep an opening at two o'clock."

"Thank you,"

and Metta Nilsen gets up and gives him an extra special little smile and says:

"I am sure that what you say counts quite a bit, too."

"Of course."

Across the square, up the steps into the kitchen at the Bus Station Cafe, where the steam from dinner preparations was hanging near the ceiling, the cook was yelling above the noise from the dish-washing, and a long line of people stood waiting at the counter. Marianna was standing there, Metta could see her through the glass door: "Can you please take over for Marianna a second, Cook? I have to talk to her."

Marianna came over, out of breath, and whispered: "It's incredible how these pigs are stuffing themselves." They both giggled and Marianna said:

"After all, I can't just lie down and cry now, can I?"

"I got an appointment for you with the Social Services Counselor. At two o'clock."

"But I can't leave work until three thirty."

"I'll take over for you."

"But . . ."

"Be there at two. He's expecting you."
"It won't work, I just know it."
"Oh, come on now."
"Don't worry. I'm not going to fall apart."
"What does Hans say about it?"
"He says . . . he doesn't really say anything."
"No, I guess he wouldn't."
"It's just as much my fault!"
"Sure. I know that. I have to go back home for a few minutes."

She poked Marianna with her elbow, the way they used to poke each other when they were balancing on a board between stacks of dirty old tires, a little reminder that things can shatter into a thousand pieces if you don't watch what you're doing, and then she disappeared

Metta Nilsen, for the man sitting in the cafe on the mountain, writing, there is nothing but fog everywhere, and there's a girl behind the counter at this cafe too, but there are almost no customers. He hunches over his notebook and writes about Marianna opening the door of the cafe and the hum of voices, umbrellas hanging on the edges of the tables, coats on the chairs, a lady eating cakes and the drawer of the cash register hopping in and out with its jingling sound.

15

The man writing rouses Henrietta Brunberg late in the morning. He lets her wake up with a throbbing pain in her large body, as if she had been drinking the previous evening. She awakens after dreaming about a bell ringing and a boat leaving the dock for the last time, while she was left standing there alone. She gets up and realizes that she is naked, sees the cut-open underwear next to the bed. The bell rings again and again. It was the doorbell that woke her up. She throws on a bathrobe, goes down the stairs, opens the door just a crack. It is the friend of the family arriving for his morning visit. "Oh, it's you. What are you doing here?"

She is standing in the middle of the floor, holding her bathrobe closed at the neck. He asks her if she's not in the mood for a visit. He will gladly sit down and wait. She pads barefoot out into the kitchen to put on the coffee. In the tiny mirror on the wall she gets a glimpse of her face, the wrinkles around the mouth and eyes. She gets a bad taste in her mouth just looking at herself: "Toads," she thinks. She wants to go upstairs and get dressed when she sees the friend of the family behind her in the mirror. He grabs her from behind, lets his hands glide down over her hips: "Yes, Henrietta, time marches on."

"Let me go," she says quietly, "let me go." When he fails to give in immediately, she removes his hands forcefully and says curtly: "I have to go up and get dressed. You watch the coffee water." So he is left standing there on the kitchen floor, but has managed to put out the cups when she comes back and he's gotten out a bottle, a draught from the big, wide world placed here just for you, Henrietta. She sits down and tastes the brew. It is sweet like a liqueur and syrupy, the bottle has broad hips. She asks him: "Do you think it is easier to get the better of me by cunning than by force?" He sighs: "No, not at all. According to Arve, it's only senior citizens that turn you on."

"Well, let me show you what turns Arve on," she says then, goes up and gets the severed underwear and holds it out for him to see. "What will he do next time? Stick the scissors into my breast?" "Oh how tragic. What bitter thoughts." The friend of the family sits and purses his lips. He taps up and down with the tip of one shoe, looks out the window and mumbles: "You can't see the ocean from here."

"What is that supposed to mean?" she says sharply, and imagines herself standing over at the window with her back turned, the day she first came here, knowing that Arve is behind her, eager to hear what she will say, and it just pops out of her, that she feels the only thing missing is that you can't see the ocean from the living room window. And that night they make love for the first time in the new house, but she can't let herself go, and he can't reach her. Finally he comes. He turns away from her unhappy.

"He was worried about you when you didn't come home yesterday evening," says the friend of the family.

"He's afraid of losing his things. Here in this house we can never throw anything away. Cardboard boxes, rags, old books. It all accumulates. I, too, am one of his many things."

"He is not happy."

"Yes, I know that, but what can I do?"

"If it's over between you, you ought to break off the relationship."

"Do you have any suggestions?"

"Take a vacation, for starters."

"School. What about the school?"

"You're not irreplaceable. Find a university student to substitute for you."

"And then what?"

"You can take a trip with the other man in your life. See what it's like."

"The other man in my life?"

she sits there looking at him with her coffee cup in her hand and it is clear to her that she will have to set things straight herself. She goes out in the kitchen to find some food, but there is nothing she feels like eating. The friend of the family has made himself comfortable in his chair. He is pouring himself small shots from the bottle. And outside, beyond the square window frame, the wind reveals the white underside of the lilac leaves, and the birch leaves go rolling along the ground, yellow and wet. When she returns to the living room, her heart is held in a clasp of iron. She pours herself a drink.

Over on the school grounds she sees a gang of boys playing ball, splashing water everywhere.

Skogmann sees a flock of boys on the school grounds playing ball, splashing water everywhere. He is sitting at the kitchen table at Krok-Anna's place and has noticed the friend of the family hopping toward the teacher's house like a sparrow in his small black shoes, trying to miss the worst puddles. The wind ripples across the pools of water, like the surface of the coffee becomes turbulent when Skogmann blows on it. Coffee disappears by the cupful into Skogmann's belly before the old man goes out on the road to fight against the wind

it is empty in the house when he gets home again and chilly in the rooms. The stove made by Trolla Stoveworks has gone out, no one has kept an eye on it while Skogmann was away. And Skogmann, fumbling around down on his knees by the open stove, thinks he has to get the house warm before Henrietta comes and picks up her suitcases. She will come soon, unless maybe she isn't even up yet. Maybe she will send her husband down after them when he gets home. But wouldn't it be reasonable for her to come herself and say thank you for taking care of her last night? In any event she will have to come down to the storekeeper's. But if he is to see her when she goes over there he'll have to make a fire in the post office which has a window facing that direction and sit at the counter with the book he's going to read. He dismisses the thought. She may do as she pleases. If she doesn't come, there is no sense in asking her to come. It was no doubt my independent position which caused her to come to me. Perhaps also because she knows I read books about a lot of issues. He doesn't light the stoves in the post office. He goes to his usual place at the table. There, between the trees in the garden, he looks out toward the sea, toward Eik Island Sound. He opens the book against the coarsely woven cloth on the table and makes notes whenever he comes to something important. But he can't manage to concentrate as well as usual. Perhaps the book is not what he was expecting. He loses himself in things which have nothing to do with the reading at hand. Memories keep surfacing, he can't repress them. He sees Henrietta's back disappearing into the darkness. A thought runs through his mind from an old book, a story about Grundtvig's mother, whatever connection there might be between her and Henrietta. On the notepad he writes with the script of an old man the assertion made by the recent hours: "Lately I have noticed many things in our area." And he looks around and discovers for the first time in many years that the room is empty and unpleasant, that the chair by the stove is crying for someone to come and sit in it. Skogmann closes the book and rests his head on his hands. He hears the wind in the background (in the walls) while the lines of Ørjasæter's "Moose" glide past: *"I often worry and wonder why I am so long-legged and ugly looking, with such utterly odd and different features; my bony legs bowed out, and my hunchback shaped quite weird, though strong as any other forest creature's, my cheeks marked with gashes and a startled stub of beard, my complexion course and grayish pale? You are so fine and lovely as a lily, little and light and frail."* Skogmann, the old postmaster is no longer sitting quietly. He is walking around in the kitchen. At that moment it seems as if he hears the screech of a heavy gate closing and he tumbles into a black abyss because, old man that he is, he is standing there thinking about another man's wife. After a while he has to go to the store to buy tobacco. He realizes that something is going on, but he is not able to say just what. *"Alone everywhere I go."*

16

Red flecks had appeared on Anna-Marja Kretsen's throat by the time she finally came down the stairs from the loft and into the kitchen where two men sat waiting for her. For her, a woman who almost never saw people except when she was shopping, whether in Ramvik or here on the island. She said that she was sorry they had to wait, but they told her they had plenty of time. One of them was the municipal engineer. And even so he wasn't aware that her husband worked in the same building he did over there on the mainland. Only then did she realize that Olver didn't have any more contact with people during the work day than she did. The municipal engineer said that there were so many people in the Big Cross that he couldn't manage to keep up with everything going on there. Everything has gotten so big that the individual is in danger of getting lost, he said. And that is a serious problem, serious. Anna-Marja thought that she had always been invisible, always hidden away since she got married, and the well-being of the individual is the goal of all social measures, said the municipal engineer.

The man who accompanied him was a younger man, sitting with a black briefcase over his knees, waiting for the municipal engineer to get done. Anna-Marja felt sorry for him because he had to sit and listen to this lecture that people were supposed to answer "yes" or "no" to off the top of their heads. To that extent she had come to her senses. And she looked at the young man's shoes. He had been walking in mud on the road on Eik Island. She was ashamed of the island, for there was no proper road here and now he had a thick border of gravel and manure drying around the edge of his shoes. And if they weren't water-tight, those shoes, well then his feet were probably wet too. And all the while the municipal engineer continued his talk because he remembered that Kretsen himself was a member of the Ramvik Labor Party, yes, he said that all the conservatives say that we in the Labor Party only think about the masses and not about the individual, but the masses, yes, who are the masses, Mrs. Kretsen, the masses are you and I, we are the ones they mean. She looked at his shoes again, those thin leather soles. What was the point of wearing such things at this time of year? He would catch cold before he got himself back to Molde or Oslo or wherever it was he came from. The municipal engineer was finally getting to the point, the heart of his errand, that he and the young gentleman would like to get some answers to a few questions, so that the municipal government can get an idea of what people in the municipality think,

Anna-Marja can no longer keep her thoughts from those shoes. She asks if he doesn't want something to dry them off with so they won't be ruined, such fine new shoes. He gets confused and looks down at his feet and excuses himself several times because he brought so much gravel in with him. Anna-Marja gets warm and blushes because he thinks that is what she is worried about. He says that he is used to travelling and if he had only known that the weather would be like this he would have worn some other shoes. The municipal engineer says that nature and climatic conditions are so varied in our elongated country. He has been many places. By then Anna-Marja has already gone after a rag. She starts wiping off the shoes, bent down close to him, and a new wave of warmth washes over her when she thinks that maybe her slip is hanging down so long that the municipal engineer can see it below her hem. She should have fixed it by tying the shoulder straps a little tighter or something, but it is too late now. What should she do? Better sit back down. Sit and pull her skirt down as far as possible. But she can't pull too hard or they will notice it. They want to get going on the questions. The young man sits down at the table and takes out his papers. "What is it like, in your opinion, living in this place? What are the greatest disadvantages about being here?" "But shouldn't you rather ask Olver about that? He works at the Big Cross, so you shouldn't have to go much out of your way." The municipal engineer says that this survey is intended primarily for the people who stay on the island all the time. Anna-Marja is requested to please answer yes or no. So she does that, all the way until it occurs to her that they are surely going to use

THE FERRY CROSSING

this for something:

"In the event that conditions are made favorable for doing so," they say, "could you consider moving nearer the municipal center?"

"We'd just as soon stay here the rest of the time, Olver and I."

"You must take into consideration that you would get a moving subsidy."

"It's too late for us to move."

"It is quite possible that Eik Island won't remain the same as it has been either. It is not beyond the realm of possibility that most people will want to leave, that the ferry will be shut down, and then it won't be so easy for people up in years to live here . . ."

"No . . ."

"So on the question about moving in the event that conditions are made favorable I think you ought to answer yes."

"You know more about it than I do, I guess," she says then and the red flecks reappear because she is afraid that she might answer something that Olver won't like, and since she doesn't know what she ought to answer she thinks it must be the best thing to stick to what the engineer says. After all, he works at the Big Cross and must know. But a tiny doubt is gnawing at her, and she thinks again and again: "I should never have gotten involved in this, I should have said no." Aloud she says, "In the event that the ferry is taken away, of course, it would not be possible to live here." And the municipal engineer says, "The wording of the question is 'in the event that conditions are made favorable' so your answer would have to be interpreted as a yes."

the young man looks at the municipal engineer for a couple of seconds before he writes down the answer. They get to more concrete questions, about annual income and children's ages. She answers and answers, all the way until they hand her the pen and ask her to sign. She is sweating and replies, "I never sign anything when my husband is not at home. Never." They try to convince her: "This is not a legal document, it is an opinion poll." They only need her signature as proof that they were here. And that her answers are correct, as far as she knows. They look impatient, so she bends over and writes: Anna-Marja Kretsen. And they pack up their papers and leave quickly. She stands and watches them go from the window. Things seem to be closing in around her, for she has promised Olver never to sign anything while he is away, and she never has up to now, she remembers that paper she signed as a young girl that Olver and she would never sell the tiny patch of ground they had gotten here to anyone who was outside the "family." But the "family"—what was that? A collection of poor folks spread around the countryside and seaside, doing carpentry work and construction, with almost nothing in common and nearly never even seeing each other. Olver is red and godless and she has to follow his lead. They own this barren place here and will be here for the duration, won't they? At least as long as she hasn't done something foolish that causes them to lose it, what with the youngest boy only being eight, how would that turn out? She had better call Olver, but on the way to the telephone she stops, because it occurs to her that the switchboard operators in the Big Cross could eavesdrop on her.

17

And the man writing is creating roads in the fog so that the blue bus from the Ramvik Bus Company can remember how to get in to Molde, jostle off down the bumpy gravel roads, stop at the milk stands and mail boxes and pick up travellers who step up on the running board and into the bus while they look around for people they know, women with scarves on their heads and umbrellas sticking up out of their handbags, but who speak softly with each other while the motor rumbles and whirs. He will have to put in a long distance call to the Norwegian Bus Owners Association to initiate negotiations on what the ride from Ramvik to Molde will cost, but he hasn't heard the result of the discussions when

Hans Kristiansson, mason's apprentice, gets off the bus at the bus station in Molde and walks to the office where his father works. "Idiot," he says mumbling to himself while he sits in the office waiting for an audience with The Great One, who is currently in a meeting. The door to the outer office is standing open, a secretary is sitting there striking the keys on a typewriter. Smeck, smeck, smeck smeck smeck. He sits looking around: it has been a long time since he was here last. The chairs have been reupholstered yet another time. The large desk is neat as always, the blinds closed. As always. He feels around his pockets for cigarettes, doesn't find any. Goes out to bum one off the secretary, a scared, little mouse, sitting there with the tips of her toes pressed against the floor, typing. She says: "He doesn't like people smoking in this office, you know. Can't you just skip it for now?" "So I'm not allowed to smoke here." Secretary: "I don't smoke here either, but . . ." "He can't forbid you to." No, he can't. She goes after her purse and gives him a pack. "You must be scared shitless of him. Sure you are, I can see it all over you, just as if he were standing behind you with a revolver. And there must be a lot to do at this time of year I would think." She is upset by such private questions and says that, of course, there is plenty to do and it's a good thing, too. "Because the slow days, when I just sit here, seem endless." "And you're probably sitting there with a bad conscience because you aren't working like a dog, even though it isn't your fault that the workload isn't dispersed evenly. And I guess you haven't found yourself a husband," he says. Oh, no she

keeps typing, astounded, stops briefly to laugh a little, but keeps typing, faster and faster, "not me, and what's it to you anyway?" "No husband, no children," says Hans. She looks anxiously at him, as if he stood ready to pounce on her: "What are you so jumpy about?" he asks. And she mumbles: "What are you talking about?"

"I'm going to have a baby. My girlfriend is going to have a baby." For a moment he is just as frightened as she is, sucks on his cigarette and retreats, but feels a kind of relief that it isn't just Marianna and Metta who know about it any more, now he also has someone on his side, this woman sitting here looking at him with her mouth half open. What is she staring at? She is a hell of a ways from being pretty, to tell the truth, with those sharp front teeth like a rat and with gray rings of sweat under the arms of her white blouse. Incredibly enough she grabs the cigarette package, lights up and whispers: "Poor you."

"Why that?" he says. "There's no reason why it should be worse for us than for anyone else." That was the truth all right, that line of thinking.

"It won't be any easier just because other people have the same problem." Something lost its grip on her, she could breathe more easily, stretch her back muscles:

"I heard the telephone conversation between your boss and your father. I couldn't avoid it when they called from Ramvik."

"What did he say?"

"He said you needed a lesson you wouldn't forget, and that he doubted you'd ever amount to anything."

"What did Dad say?"

"He agreed with him."

But then they hear voices out in the corridor and she quickly returns to her typing. The Great One is finished with his conference. She places the ashtray with the two butts in a drawer, hides the cigarette package, concentrates on the letter she is working on. He says: "If you need to work now, then you can't talk to me," but then he hears his father's voice outside, confident and self-righteous, like his own; it is enough to make you hurt. Any minute now he'll be face to face with an older edition of himself. He feels tired, empty. He grasps at a way out, the only one he can see in this town: "Elina, I'm coming by your place tonight. Can you lend me ten crowns?" She looks at him and doesn't understand what he means, but out there a hand has already been placed on the knob, but she whispers yes anyway and starts typing as if possessed, for it is only seconds before the Great Karl Johan Kristiansson will open the door and walk in.

18

He just doesn't think it's fair, the man writing, so he calls up the man at the Bus Owners' Association and says that 6 crowns and 40 øre is too much for the bus fare from Ramvik to Molde, and do they think people take the bus for their health on those bumpy roads, is that what they think? But the man in Oslo hangs up and nothing can be done about it. Back at his table he tries to calm down by placing a man by the name of

Arve Brunberg at a desk on one of the upper floors in the Big Cross and directing his red-rimmed gaze at the gray expanse out toward Eik Island, toward the dark rocks jutting up and the wooden houses like small boxes between them. The heather red and brown, wind-blown clumps of trees here and there, the sea churning all around, the ferry tossing on the waves in the middle of the fjord. Far beneath him down on the asphalt people bend into the wind and hold onto their headgear as they walk along,

he has placed his watch in front of him on the desk. He tries to concentrate so that he can *see* the hour hand on the clock move, but his eyes close while he is staring and he fantasizes or thinks of things he has learned here and there that he can use to help him find himself again. This man who cannot even save his own family situation will instead save Eik Island. He will get to the bottom of the whole mess and show them, and especially Henrietta. He will show her what it is to see the ocean. But his sleepless night keeps catching up with him, time and again he jerks awake, he sees Henrietta pressing her naked thighs around the loins of a strange man, tossing her head back and screaming, screaming,

one of the girls at the counter comes in with a document he is supposed to sign and stops in the doorway when he grabs the edge of the desk with both hands and cries: "No!" She looks at him, startled, and says: "My God, Brunberg, I think you must be sick. Wouldn't you rather take the ferry home and go to bed?" He says: "No way. I was just up working all night on something I had to finish,"

and out there in the reception area a man is waiting to talk to him. She asks him if she should show him in or ask him to come back another day. "Let him in," says Brunberg, "that's what I'm sitting here for," and a little, crooked man comes in. He has hung up his coat outside, but carries his hat in his hand as if he were afraid that someone would steal it from him. He stops over by the door and Arve Brunberg has to point to the chair before the man understands that he is supposed to sit down. He is the fellow who lost most of his hearing one day when he was standing in a rock quarry and one of the blasts went haywire and now he is beating down every door in the place trying to find out if the National Social Security Administration and the others in there are going to respond to his request for disability payments. He asks if it isn't possible to be more insistent, reminds them that he cannot work any longer, that he needs the money right away, and he hides his blown-apart hands in his jacket pockets in order not to make a bad impression on the elegant man behind the desk.

"We'll just have to take it easy and wait," says Arve Brunberg. "Everything in its own time."

The face on the other side of the desk does not change its expression, displays its same friendly countenance. The head stretches forward and tries to comprehend.

"There is nothing we can do but wait. There is no doubt that you are perfectly entitled to compensation."

The man catches the word "wait," and argues that life has to go on, he has bills to pay and repairs to make on his house:

"There is nothing else to do but wait!" The man shrugs his shoulders, Brunberg grabs his desk calendar, pages feverishly to the next month, tears out a date page and jots a note on the backside: "Come again on this date."

The girl at the reception desk comes in: "Was there something you wanted, Brunberg? I could hear you shouting."

"I am just trying to get him to understand that there is nothing we can do but wait!" She shows the man out. He is shaking his head and Brunberg roars after him: "There is nothing we in this office can do. Please understand that!" Sure, sure. It makes no difference who we place the blame on. He leans back in his chair, back into the days when their little girl was big enough that he and Henrietta could be alone together in the living room in the late afternoons when he came home from work,

they no longer have anything to talk about. Their first big stint has been completed, their finances are going fine, there is not anything to say except that here they sit. They had expected a life of shared pleasures. But there is very little to share. The surrounding community seems far away. Henrietta: "Well, here we sit!" He has nothing to add. Henrietta creeps into her books, those damned history books she has ordered from all over creation. He sits and looks at her. Or goes out on the steps, or lies down on the sofa with a magazine or a book. He gets more and more tired and that's how the hours pass. Their daughter stays out of the house because she has long ago understood what is going on and stays away so she won't be dragged into anything,

but he will not admit that anything is going on. Henrietta:

"We don't talk to each other any more."

"Don't we talk to each other?"

"We don't talk to each other like we used to."

"We can't go around playing newlyweds all the time!"

"No, but I had thought that . . ."

"I'm doing just fine."

"Are you really?"

"Yes, I'm satisfied with my life."
"Maybe I'm the only one who expects too much."

19

Then she leans back in her chair. That's where it stops—they pull the big curtains across the window when evening comes, close the drapes on their happy private life in a new and spacious house. They can't see the ocean from the chairs where they are sitting, who needs to? But when Henrietta goes up to the second floor and stands gazing out in a fogless autumn evening without turning on the light up there and sees hundreds of shimmering lanterns out there in the skerries, he doesn't have the courage to walk over to her and say what he would like to:

"You damned romantic!"

He goes quietly downstairs again and puts on a record, perhaps a bit on the loud side, to remind her that he exists, but the problems are never mentioned, they just sit there waiting for things to fall into place by themselves, expecting that one evening they will suddenly start laughing. They visit other people very seldom in this period, feel they should set things straight between themselves before they seek out their friends, or at least they each believe that the other feels this way. Because they can't talk about this either. He is the most scared. He can't bear the thought that they might actually become enemies, he doesn't dare imagine that things might not turn out as they had thought, for there is not much else than the remnants of an old love holding them together. Not interests, not money—they can both manage quite well on their own, not their child, who is more and more capable of getting along without them, not this island—they aren't from here—and that's why he has to deny it, deny it categorically if she comes out and says that not everything is as it should be. One day in the spring

a letter arrives from the military. He has been summoned for reserve duty. He is sitting there turning the brown envelope around in his hand at the kitchen table. He is to be away from her for three weeks, for the first time since they got married. He says to the woman standing over at the stove that it will be lonely for her, this separation. But then she replies that maybe it will be good for them both. He asks what she means by that.

Nothing more than that in all marriages there comes a day when being eternally new for the other person no longer happens automatically. From that day forth a little wound has opened and lies there smarting, day in and day out; that he cannot totally depend on her, but he cannot say anything directly, never, his way of dealing with things is that never an unkind word should be spoken between them, he would rather show her by indirect means if he wished something to be different, for between people who live in such close contact with each other movements and expressions end up being the only viable language, words will always lie there and rot between them once they've been said, and the hour hand on the clock,

it moves ahead at a snail's pace, he was watching it with both eagerness and trepidation for in a very short time he can leave the office and think: "I did not give out this day either." He started working on plans to not show up, to frighten her by disappearing for a day or two, after all he didn't have to be at work again before Monday. It might help her understand if he withdrew like a sick animal and suffered alone. Was there anyone he could visit? No one. He would have to go to a hotel. And he

heads right to the weekend ads in the newspaper for package deals with a bar and dance floor and an informal, carefree milieu, but stops at the word "dance" and glances down at his business suit. He realizes how he will appear on a Saturday night on the town with the knees of his trousers bagging out over at the bar while happy, party-clad and well-groomed people laugh their way past him. He knew that he could never do it and what would he have achieved by it? She would surely be pleased if he stayed away.

It wasn't his style. He wasn't like that. He wasn't the type to run away. He would rather face the music. He remembered the date he had made with Olver Kretsen when they left the Bus Station Cafe early that morning, that Olver would come to his house, so they could talk about the business with that boat. He had latched onto Olver to avoid spending the evening alone with Henrietta. And this man who was not the master of his own fate, was grabbing the reins of the tiny society he lived in. He may have known that this was important, but he did not realize that it was his first lucid moment in a long time.

Out in the bathroom he rubs his face with cold water and waits until it dries off by itself. He lights a cigarette and notes that he is staggering a bit as he walks back through the corridor. As he is about to enter his office the elevator passes by on its way up and with amazement he catches sight of the head of Marianna Kretsen, but the elevator does not stop. He is thinking faster than his skull can tolerate, runs up the stairs next to the elevators and sees Marianna walking slowly down the corridor. He calls after her, as she is searching for a number on a door. She turns around, startled: "Marianna! You must be looking for your father, but he isn't up here. He usually works in the basement, if he doesn't have something special to do other places in the building."

Marianna stands and looks at him, but doesn't answer.

"Or were you looking for me maybe? You went one floor too far if you were."

She just stands there.

"But it was probably your father you wanted. He's downstairs, like I said."

"Can't I go anywhere I want to?"

"What?"

"Isn't this a public building?"

"Of course," he says quietly, "I thought you had gotten lost and so I just..."

he turns around slowly and walks back the way he came. The receptionist is standing in the doorway looking for him. "Where have you been? There's a phone call for you."

"I'm coming."

It is Henrietta.

"So you're up already!"

"I don't sleep as soundly as you think."

(and he hears the record player in the background)

"Sounds like you even have people there to help you stay awake!"

"Yes, we have a permanent visitor around this place."

"Oh, him. If it's *conversation* you want, he's just the man."

"He is the one who asked me to call you and ask you to bring home some beer."

"Is Brunberg's refrigerator already empty?"

"The evening is young, Brunberg."

(Shit, she's already drunk.)

"Shouldn't you invite Skogmann over too? Then it would really be lively!"

"He is against strong drink."

"Yes, but he probably has his *forte* in other areas."

"Our friend of the family would like to speak to you, Arve."

He can tell she doesn't find this entertaining any more,

"Tell him to keep his seat. I'll get the beer. Listen, promise me one thing: that you won't go out."

"Oh, dear, just when I was planning to go from door to door and announce how horrible you are to me."

"Go right ahead. Then we wouldn't have anything to hide."

He hangs up.

It starts raining again outside,

the sky has clouded over

so it is like twilight,

he sits, holding his head, unable to work. They are closing up the reception area. The girl is coming in to do the filing for the day.

"You must be sick today, Brunberg."

"Sit down, Anni, I need to talk to someone."

"I have to close up first, you know."

"Close down the whole mess."

She comes and sits down and lights a cigarette.

"Is it your wife, Brunberg?"

"Yes, dammit. It's a tough situation."

"You've got to straighten things out. You haven't been yourself for some time."

"What am I supposed to do? She's completely screwed up."

"And you're not."

"That's not the point. We have nothing to talk about,"

he turns his chair around and looks out the window,

but what does he see? he sees the sea

and it is beginning to take on a rosy glow out there, this sea of his; he feels lethargic from too little food and too many cigarettes, too many thoughts and no actions, he sits there blinking at something far away, so lethargic that he can barely manage to conjure up a desperate vision of Henrietta and her antics with the friend of the family,

he can barely get them up the stairs to the second floor, unbuttoning their buttons, entering the bedroom where they slip the clothes off of each other and get underway,

but he is too lethargic to keep up with them, poor Brunberg, he really doesn't give a damn, he's so burned out, he only sees himself coming down the stairs from the floor above where he tried to show Marianna Kretsen which way to go, he sees himself at the bar of the weekend hotel, he sees the suit he has on wherever he goes, a gray suit for the office, a gray suit for men of his age, for those who have worked in an honest manner throughout their youth and whose hair has, little by little, become thin, who don't owe anyone anything, who are well off, relatively, but haven't got the remotest possibility of advancement.

"You must enjoy seeing the boss down and out."

"I wouldn't imagine you are any different on the inside than other men. I don't think you're anything out of the ordinary."

"No, and I'm so gray. Could you, for example, possibly imagine . . ."

She sits there looking at him for a long time and he hears her say:

"When men like you have problems they can never imagine that there is anything wrong with them other than a lack of young women."

20

In the hallway upstairs Marianna Kretsen is trying to collect herself after Brunberg has disappeared. She looks around before she knocks. She stands there while her knuckles beat against the door.

She wonders if she could manage if it weren't for Metta, and whether it was a defeat to have told her about this,

while the man inside holds out his hand to shake hers. Maybe there isn't so much to talk about. He asks her why she hasn't discussed this with her parents: "Your father is not so narrow-minded. He can take it." But she says she wants to go it on her own and that it is his duty to remain silent.

He tells her what the usual procedure is for such cases. Mentions a doctor who may be willing to do the operation. It seems unreal. She forgets for a while that she's the one they are discussing and not someone else. Finally he accompanies her out into the corridor and says, "Good luck," like any normal human being. She feels happy.

Somebody is on her side. She glides down the stairs and runs across the square to Metta and tells her how relieved she feels. Metta is talking on the phone and hangs up as soon as Marianna comes. "Bye, Hans."

"Why did you hang up, Metta?"

"I felt you have enough of your own troubles without having to listen to other people's."

"What are you talking about?"

"He was fired from his job."

Marianna grabs for the receiver, but drops it again. She doesn't know where to call.

"He is in Molde."

"What's he doing there?"

"Trying to talk some sense into his father. Go on home now. We can talk this evening."

Marianna walks slowly down the stairs, to the place where she is allowed to be, to wait. That's really the only thing that room in the basement is, a waiting room, and she has nothing else to do but wait.

21

while the man writing shows the municipal engineer for Ramvik into the home of Karl Magnus Skogmann by the ferry landing on Eik Island and lets him motion to the other man with him to be seated, which inspires Skogmann to remain standing stubbornly and look out the window with his hands behind him and allow his irritation to increase over the gestures they are making behind his back. When the municipal engineer is finished explaining what their errand is, he asks if he may use the telephone to call his office and Skogmann says:

"Be my guest. There it is. It was the Germans, by the way, who laid the telephone cable out here to Eik Island."

The municipal engineer puts down the receiver. "What are you talking about?"

"I am talking about how it was the Germans who stretched the telephone cable across Eik Island Sound, put up poles along the road here and rolled out the wire all the way out to the portable telephones they had in their bunkers out on the island."

"I'm afraid I don't know what you are getting at," says the municipal engineer, but at that moment they answer over at the Big Cross and he speaks softly and quickly into the receiver, as if he were giving orders, and Skogmann picks up the papers they have brought along and begins to look through them, his yellow index finger moves along the stenciled page right down to the dotted line for the signature, full name. Then he walks over to the window again and says: "I see that you want to get people to sign here saying that they will voluntarily move away from here. You'll have a hard time getting my signature on that,"

and he is told something about a large shipworks that may be set up and that it will be necessary to move some of those who live around the harbor on Eik Island, everything in its time, of course, but the directors and technical staff have had to maintain confidentiality up to now, we had to first see what could be done here, before we started making predictions about the future, and we had to avoid conflict, such that the firm in question wouldn't pack up their blueprints and start looking for another location. Skogmann looks out.

"What can I say? My rooms will be vacant in the not so distant future anyway. But move away from here I will not."

"You as a former civil servant will surely not wish to throw a wrench into the works for the municipality?"

"You'll have to convince me that this will make people happy."

"We can't afford to pass up this offer. It's not every remote village that gets an offer of this sort."

"You won't get me to sign, before I get some real answers."

"Don't you have confidence that your municipal government does its best in everything?"

"Oh, they sit over there in the Big Cross and shuffle papers that people don't get to look at, or else they're written in languages people can't read."

"Speaking of the Big Cross . . . the municipality can't afford to pay for all that grandeur, unless we get a few more wheels turning!"

"So why do they build these monstrosities?"

"We are not always our own boss, Skogmann. There are other interests to be represented."

"We got our municipal autonomy back in 1837, as I recall."

"Yes, you know your history, Skogmann, but that law was never more than a piece of paper."

"A piece of paper stating that they can do as they please, they'll never get that from me."

"I never thought you'd be the person to cripple the Ramvik municipality with unfounded suspicions about a new project."

"And I had confidence they would govern the way people wanted."

"The people's opinion is exactly what we want on this survey."

"And that's why you're giving them the answer yourself!"

"Today, Skogmann, the two biggest property owners have declared themselves willing to relinquish their properties according to the assessment . . ."

"I refuse to sign anything I don't know the full details on."

"We'll have to manage without your signature."

"You just do that."

"Goodbye, Skogmann."

"Goodbye, Mr. Engineer."

Skogmann is left standing over by the window with his hands at his sides. The people over at the store see the municipal engineer come flying out of the house with his overcoat unbuttoned, trying to hold it closed by making fists in each pocket and pressing them together. They say: "The municipal engineer has now been to see Skogmann." And Skogmann sees a gull trying to cling to a telephone post in the wind. Afterwards it is as though he lowers the shades and collapses inwardly. It is as if

people were standing outside the door to the post office, cleaning off their shoes, people who want to come in and hear what is in the newspapers he reads, and when he has told them, they take their hats and caps and leave without a sound.

He wakes up and shakes his head because he is apparently able to sleep on his feet like a horse in the middle of the day, but everything was so lifelike that he has to go out into the post office to make certain that the outer door is locked. Henrietta's suitcases are out there, she must be coming soon to pick them up. The wind nips at the siding, it is cold and blustery, he turns around and goes back into the living room,

to the book about social democratic perspectives, which he sits down and looks through for a sentence he can hang onto for dear life. But he soon finds that he cannot absorb this language, gets up from his chair, goes over to the telephone and starts calling around to various people on the island,

22

the man writing hears the telephone ringing in the houses all around and sees the receivers being lifted off the hooks. Skogmann makes his round. But he is too late to catch Anna-Marja Kretsen, she's already out on the road, her skirt glued to her body by the wind, she walks bent forward and people sitting in their houses along the road say: "Gosh, it's already two. There goes Anna-Marja to the school to wash floors." She is wearing rubber boots like a man, with a scarf over her mouth, walking fast, although there is no rush now. She is walking to the job she has taken on,

but when she comes into one of the two classrooms in the school and sees her own muddy footprints behind her, it occurs to her that there is no need to wash today because there hasn't been any school since she washed yesterday. The children haven't been here, the room is clean. The desk tops gleam at her, the chairs are neatly arranged, the chalk tray by the teacher's desk is empty and dusted. In the little side room the rag for washing the floor is hung to dry over the rim of the wash-bucket and the broom is leaning in the corner, ready for use. But she can't start washing all over again. She usually spends a good hour at the school before she goes home and puts on dinner for Olver. Now she sees two women coming up the road from the storekeeper's and she can't go out now and meet them, because what if they don't know that there was no school today and think she is shirking her work since she is going home so early. Or even worse, maybe they think she is getting paid for a job she doesn't do. She hears the outer door blow open and knows that will reveal that she is there, but she can't go out and shut it again, because what would she say then? What if they see her and come in to talk to her and discover that she is just sitting there not doing anything at all? What will she say then?

she sits motionless on one of the low chairs so they won't see her through the window and hopes that they will soon be past, but when she stretches her neck to check that they are well on down the road, she sees them lifting the latch on the gate and coming onto the playground where the kids usually play ball. She runs to the little room, fills the bucket with water, squirts some detergent into it, and when they reach the doorway she is busy pushing the mop into all the corners with her upper body bent over and pressed hard against the mop handle.

"Bless hard work!" they say and stand there with their shopping bags, inspecting the room. She straightens up. "We wanted to find out if the municipal engineer has been at your place," and she knew immediately that they knew he had been there earlier in the day,

"everyone was wondering if you had signed. We wanted to ask you if you signed."

She answers that since they begged her to, she did sign, but only to attest that the information she had given them was correct,

"Oh, no," they complain, she has also signed that she will allow herself to be moved from the island whenever they want to do it. Whatever that is all about, she'll find out soon enough, but Skogmann has been down at the store and said that nobody should sign, and that's just what they had thought themselves. She stands at the window watching them as they continue up the road, wringing her hands. The wind blew all the warmth out of her when she walked over; now she has waves of heat rippling down her back and she doesn't know what to do. At that moment she spots the municipal engineer coming out of Krok-Anna's house. In a few minutes he will pass by the school,

she stands helpless, looking at the washing equipment, but manages to collect everything and put it back in the cabinet. She puts on her coat again and goes out to wait by the gate until the engineer and the man with him come past.

23

Henrietta Brunberg's friend of the family strolls around the floor of the teacher's house, whistling to a new record he has put on. Henrietta is lying in a chair with her hands and feet dangling: "Come here. You may as well keep me company since you're here anyway." She has very gradually begun to lose contact with her surroundings, but he isn't listening to her. She keeps on talking to herself about Arve and everything. "Who knows? Maybe it will get better tomorrow. Sure. In a year. Come home from school and hang around waiting for him to come over on the ferry. We sit down at the dinner table and he asks for the salt. Then it gets very quiet in here. Damned quiet.

"Sure, I can go it alone. Hand in my resignation now and maybe stop teaching already at Christmas. They can't force me to stay. If I don't want to, nobody can force me to stay. And I don't think I'm too old to meet somebody new, do you? Come here and tell me I'm still attractive. That's why you came over here today. You think I just jump in bed with anyone at all, now that my marriage is falling apart. To hell with men, all of them. You don't know the first thing about women. What is happening to me? Is this some kind of panic? Is there something wrong with realizing that time is running short?"

"Well, I'll be damned, I think someone is coming over here," says the friend of the family suddenly from over by the window. "Henrietta, there are people coming here."

The telephone rings.

"You get it," she says. "I'm tired and I want to go and lie down."

"Didn't you hear me? I said there are people coming over here."

"Yes, but answer the phone first."

It's Skogmann.

"Oh, hello. I just dropped by. Henrietta is not feeling well. But I'm sure she'll come to the phone, since it's you."

"Hello, Skogmann. I'll come and get my suitcases soon. *I* certainly don't intend to sign any papers. No municipal engineer is going to set foot in this place. No other men either. It's looking bad for them, Skogmann. No signature. I'll do as you say. You are the only person I can depend on. But there is nothing wrong in realizing that time is running short, Skogmann!"

Over at the schoolyard gate Anna-Marja Kretsen is waiting for the two men who are approaching. They are talking to each other as they walk, half shouting in order to be heard above the wind. She is waiting there for them, holding on to the gate, thinking: "If I can set this straightened out, if I can just get that paper back, I'll have achieved more than I would have thought I could today. . ." They say a quick hello and intend to just keep walking, but she goes up to talk to them, tells them that she wants to take back what she said that morning, "I have absolutely promised my husband that I would not sign anything while he is away. I beg you to let me keep that paper until tomorrow, and then it can be sent over to you, because I simply cannot sign something like that when my husband isn't here."

They have no time to discuss it now. "We have a few more houses to visit before we leave. You may call tomorrow, Mrs. Kretsen, if there is a change you would like to make . . ."

"I can't vouch for what I have signed as long as my husband hasn't seen it. Can't it be scratched out until then . . .?"

"We are coming back over here on the weekend! (How ridiculous can you get.) Excuse me, Mrs. Kretsen, but you act like you had signed your own death sentence! It is only an opinion survey, like I said. Not binding in any way. We are running late." They tear themselves away and keep walking. She's left standing, watching them as they hurry over toward the teacher's house and disappear around the back side. She's left behind and has to go home and

"Now I'm going to go to bed," says Henrietta. She hears him asking her if he should open the door or not and says he should do whatever he wants, she isn't going to talk to them. He goes out and locks the door, she goes up to her room, for he has promised her that he won't leave before Arve comes, and before lying down she stands there looking and looking out at

the chaotic stretch of sea, the gray waves breaking over the skerries, the wall of fog a bit further out, and she dives into bed, just as the telephone starts to ring. The friend of the family doesn't answer it, he can't because the two men are standing out on the steps, ringing the doorbell, and the telephone rings and rings, and they ring and ring as though they will never stop,

but it does stop, whether because she has fallen asleep or because the intruders have given up, it finally gets quiet.

24

Find someplace for Olver Kretsen to work down there in the basement of the new City Hall in Ramvik, where there is light, but not daylight. A white light emitting from long tubes in the cement corridors, between the bundles of cables and the large pipes, where he is supposed to clean up and keep things running. He has his routine duties, heating, the electrical network, and temperature control. The entire basement is filled with a steady and continual hum from the electric generator, which gradually seeps into his head and stays trapped there until he gets about halfway across the fjord on his way home on the ferry.

Now he is sitting in the little cubbyhole he has all to himself with a table and chair and a telephone and a signal panel that lights up when someone in the upper floors needs him. Occasionally there is work for him up there. But most of the time he slinks around here by himself, it doesn't bother him really, even though he liked it better when the Big Cross was still under construction and he got to be outdoors and put up cement forms along with the others, people like himself.

He has a cheap portable radio standing next to him, a prize he won at a fair in Molde a few years ago, in a giant raffle where they drew the winners the evening after he and Anna-Marja had gone back home, but the radio arrived by bus, it sure did,

now he sits listening to the news, as he often does, to keep up with the current events in the world in case he should get into a conversation with someone on the ferry on the way home. He doesn't give a hoot what happens in foreign countries and just concentrates on the domestic news, for there is so little you can do about the foreign countries anyway. He remembers what he hears and can repeat it without inserting any of his own opinions, for personal opinions have become a strictly private matter for him with the passing years. He learned early on to keep his mouth shut.

"Jesus Christ, just listen how they talk about the expansion of the provincial economy on the local channel," he thinks, "and that guy is supposed to be a member of the Labor Party, but there's no way in hell of telling him from anybody else these days, but then on the other hand the Socialist People's Party is a party for teachers, and the communists don't even have anyone on the ballot in the Ramvik elections, and that's probably smart of them, for they wouldn't be elected anyway." Politics is politics and it ought to be enough to keep up your union dues,

you used to pay them to the Workman's Association, before, that was a good group, but now its The Municipality, and they have meetings and stuff, with all the people who work for the municipality. He was at a meeting here last year,

there were only a dozen people there, when there should have been ten times that many, and the man from the central office had come to tell about the new wage agreement and get them to vote yes, and not a single one of these idiots says a word, there is total silence after the presentation, until finally the man behind him starts to clap and they sit there clapping and clapping, all of them, and he sneaks out and swears that he will never go to another of those meetings again, they might just as well not be organized at all as to be organized like sheep, but he doesn't cancel his membership,

and now he's on the last hour of the workday when Anna-Marja calls him on the telephone and he is surprised when he hears her voice, because she doesn't usually call him at work. Now she is out of breath and speaking loudly: "I have done something terrible, Olver. You must come home and straighten it out."

"Now, now, what is going on, dear?"

"I can't very well talk about it on the phone."

"There's nobody listening here, for goodness sake, just tell me."

and he hears her going on about a paper she has signed for the municipal engineer, she doesn't know how she could have done it, and now he has to come home and help her. He says that she should have supper ready and waiting for him when he comes on the ferry. Goodbye. Goodbye. At that very moment he hears that the island is being mentioned on the radio and he turns it up. There is a foreign shipbuilding firm which, through its Norwegian division, has contacted Ramvik municipality to see if there is a location suitable for a large wharf and they selected Eik Island, because everything is ideal for building docks in the harbor there, but nothing has been decided yet, no, nothing, and

this report has entered a good many ears in the upper levels in the Big Cross; Olver comes up from his basement, people are standing around in the corridors discussing it, the local newspapers are calling up, but the mayor is in Oslo at a meeting and the municipal engineer who has all the documents in the case is not available today, and everybody is claiming to know more than everybody else, but nobody wants to make a definite statement,

25

and the man writing takes in the cryptic message through the loud speaker on the wall of the cafe where he is sitting and thinking that he had better get out of there soon. But first he has to mention

Marianna who is sitting in her basement apartment waiting for yet another afternoon to pass. And it will be many more days before she gets an answer from a committee of two or three men, who will determine what her future will be like. She sees them gathered around the table where her body is lying, sees how they scrutinize every part of it, how they take her life history bit by bit and analyze it, and finally answer the question: to lock her up with a child and social security payments or to clean out a thumb-sized embryo from her womb. She leans back against the couch with her clothes on and feels her stomach, ever so carefully, and fantasizes about how her life will turn out,

she sees a crib with white spindles placed below the window in the crowded basement room, she sees herself hanging up clotheslines in the damp washroom for drying tiny baby clothes, or maybe out in the garden behind the house—a line stretched from tree to tree with the blessings of her landlords—out there where the wind now gusts across the wet, grayish yellow grass on the lawn. She knows that no one will come to see her except her father; Metta will move to another town, her mother will call her on the phone. Or maybe she herself will go home to Eik Island and move into one of the rooms in the loft beneath the newly shingled roof. Maybe she will remain there for the rest of her life and the jerky, confused movements of her mother will gradually be transferred to her, along with the conviction that she is always a burden for others and there is nothing to be done about it, no

it mustn't happen, it must not happen!

She has to get them to understand that she cannot have a baby at this point. She remembers a girl at the Folk High School, where everything was so bright and beautiful, who went with a sailor to his room one weekend when she had said that she was going home for a visit. When she found out that she was pregnant, she went to some fool who was in love with her and borrowed money for a trip to Oslo and a few hundred extra for a quack who scraped out the fetus. She came back and got a job in a little store and never talked about it any more, until one evening long afterwards when they told her she'd better watch out so she didn't get into trouble again, but she went out with the man anyway because, she said: "It doesn't matter. I can't have any children anyway." The scoundrel who had done her such a favor and taken her money had also managed to ruin her body for good,

Marianna thinks: "It's no use, it's no use," and starts calculating how she can get enough money together,

on the radio, broadcasting with its scratchy voice, she hears something about Eik Island and Ramvik. In another situation she would have listened to what they were talking about since it's her island, her town, but not today. And when you get right down to it she shouldn't have thrown away her youth in this little cafe,

"because there are other things I want to do,"

but she doesn't know for sure what they are, other than a vague idea about a job in Oslo. She knows many others who go there not knowing any more than she does. But she doesn't really know much; it's Metta who keeps informed about things, Metta who is active in politics, and Metta who can talk to anyone without feeling stupid. Metta is the one who tells her not to go around making excuses for herself all the time, "Marianna, don't go acting as if you are nothing, do what you want to," and invites her to join their study circle in the Socialist Youth Association. But Marianna says: "I don't have a head for things like that. And I don't know if I want to know any more about politics either, because it has nothing to do with me,"

"Are you sure about that?" asks Metta and squeezes one of her eyes shut, but she doesn't nag about it; Metta never nags. "But I'm the one the boys like most, because I don't have such a sharp tongue." Which is why Metta is always a bit left out in Ramvik, despite the fact that she is attractive. She is too old, yes, that's it. Girls of her type don't settle down here, they usually move away as soon as they are finished with school, or a few of them get married to the guys who work in the Big Cross and disappear into the newly built apartment houses with their dinner preparations and child rearing. Metta couldn't stand to be friends with them,

Marianna is thinking and the radio is playing records, oh God, sentimental music that she cannot stand to listen to, but doesn't want to turn off either, and what they are singing about is not this world, but something resembling it, something safe and good, and Marianna curls up wishing for something good and warm to creep inside of, something soft to put her head next to and rest alongside of, and she hears the landlady walking on the floor up above—there are only the two of them in the house—and Marianna knows she could have gone and talked to her and she would have been understanding. But Marianna doesn't want to be a burden for anyone else and decides she had better get up or she'll lie there the rest of her life. She goes out into the tiny hallway to look in the closet and see if she has anything to wear this evening,

26

but the man writing looks at his watch and lets Hans Kristiansson do the same as he emerges from his father's office; it is nearly three o'clock. He begins to wonder if he should go back to Ramvik for the night. Maybe I can explain to Marianna how things are and that I cannot help her. He thinks for a while that, if the child were born anyway, then perhaps he wouldn't have the right to call himself the father, but he soon dismisses the thought because the possibility is so remote: he wanders along the street from his father's office and down Storgata, looks in the windows he is all too familiar with; these miserable little merchants always have their innards on display, he thinks, trying to glean what little income they can from petty sales, a tiny shop with screws and buttons and needles on one side of the street, and another one with fish hooks and rain gear, and on the other side are the barbers and the booksellers. He has a ten crown piece and goes over to the Telegraph Office on Gottfried Lie's Plass and asks for the number of the

Bus Station Cafe, because he wants to talk to Marianna.

But she isn't there.

He wanders around in the streets a while and tries to find someone he knows, so he can borrow a few crowns, but they are all at work, the jerks, and don't come out when one of their friends needs them. He doesn't think about the fact that he hasn't lived here for three or four years and a lot may have changed. He stands and looks at his reflection in a window for a while to be sure that he isn't embarking on some great crisis. He seems to be the same as ever,

at any rate he feels hungry and wonders for a moment if he should go home to his mom and charm something out of her behind the back of his father, who has refused him help. But he needs to make it on his own,

he has to.

After a while he goes back to the Telegraph Office and places a call to Marianna's landlord's number, and gets her on the line, but her voice is distant, thin as a splinter. He says: "I'm in one hell of a mess now, Marianna. I've been fired." She says: "Metta told me." He says: "I can't take the responsibility of helping you with a kid." She says: "That's o.k., I wasn't planning on asking you to." He says: "That's a rotten way of putting it." She says: "I know you don't care about me. I'll manage on my own." He says: "You've got to try to get rid of the thing,"

she is standing there at the other end of the line stretched between the Telegraph Office in Molde and Ramvik, a wire that hurtles from pole to pole along the same road the busses take. She feels a prickling sensation in her body when he says: "You've got to try to get rid of..." She wants to hang up without talking about it any more, but she pulls herself together: "It ought to be my own decision, what I do. From now on." She hears him cursing under his breath, away from the receiver, and in a while he says: "It is not just your decision. As the father I have a right to help you decide." She answers that as long as he can't take his share of the responsibility for a child, he has no right to make any part of the decision, to which he shouts, "why the hell can't you give me a break?" But she says: "I don't have the energy to talk about this any more," and hangs up,

the landlady is standing in the kitchen washing dishes, Marianna thinks that maybe she has heard everything, but she doesn't have the energy to think about that either, so she goes down to her room and lays her head against the divan to do some thinking, and her thoughts seem to sing,

"What has gotten into you, Marianna, did you really think you could get any help from a guy who has always managed to get away with anything, and be admired for it to boot? While she is lying there deciding not to ever have anything to do with Hans Kristiansson again,

and not with any of the others who are playing tug-of-war with her to get her to go where they want, all those people who want to make up her mind for her, that young, beautiful, wonderful and helpless Marianna,

Hans is standing in the phone booth cursing at the dead receiver, but he has to get out because they are already announcing on the loud speaker: "Ramvik, four crowns and fifty øre." He goes to the counter and pays for the call before he realizes that he could have run out without paying and not gotten caught,

and out on the street he realizes that he has to get to Ramvik to talk some sense into her, get her to see what a difficult position he's in, and he thinks that maybe she is the only one who can help him out of this whole mess. He walks quickly, getting wet in the rain, passes a used-car lot and suddenly he is struck by a great idea. He goes in.

A man is bending over measuring the air in the tires of a Volkswagen and Hans comes up behind him:

"I need some wheels. Got anything suitable?"

The man looks up, puckers his mouth and lets out an audible sigh.

"Could I try out this one over here?"

"You'll have to hurry. We're closing in an hour."

"You could let me keep it until tomorrow, I should think."

The man thinks about it and goes through a door into the office. "Kristiansson's son is here and wants to know if he can have the Mercedes until tomorrow."

The other man comes out and looks at him.

"I have to go to Ramvik this evening and was wondering if I could have the Mercedes until tomorrow."

Another sigh. "Can we count on you to bring it back?"

"I guess that's a risk you'll just have to take."

"May I have a look at your license?"

"All right. The tank is half full. If you decide you don't want the car, you pay for the gas."

"I don't know if this is the one I want, but I do want to buy a car."

O.K. He takes the keys, they say they want him back in one piece at 9 tomorrow morning, he asks if it's necessary to come that early, but they say there are plenty of others who want to test-drive used cars on a Saturday,

he gets in and slams the door, starts the engine and lets the car lunge out of the building, so fast they have to jump back, and glancing into the mirror he sees that they are looking at each other and shaking their heads. He drives calmly down the street and smiles to himself: "You got to them that time." He feels his mood brightening, the further he gets from the center of town. Along Frænavegen as the needle on the speedometer glides up and hovers at the 90 kilometer mark. The town he grew up in disappears behind him.

27

Meanwhile, the man writing sees Olver Kretsen walk into the Bus Station Cafe in Ramvik and sit down by the window. Metta comes over to him and says that Marianna has left work earlier today because she isn't feeling well. He says Marianna ought to come home if she is sick enough to have to stay in bed. It would be a good thing for her mother. It is still a half hour until the ferry leaves,

there comes Arve Brunberg in through the door noisily lugging a case of beer. People notice him, they are familiar with him and his position.

They sit silently and look over at the island, they can barely make it out in the grayness. They think about what they have heard on the radio, but nobody brings up the topic. Not now. Arve Brunberg feels the tiredness seeping into him, Olver is thinking about his phone conversation with Anna-Marja. The door of the cafe is constantly opening, people are going in and out, the two men put on their coats to start down to the dock. The cars stream into the parking lot where they are left to wait, and the people go onboard. They are headed for Eik Island, Land Island and Vind Island. "Shall I give you a hand with the beer case?" Olver asks, but Arve wants to carry it alone. It is raining again, beating against the wall of the waiting room, against the planking on the pier and the metal roof of the ferry lying there restless on the choppy waves. Most of the passengers are down in the salon talking about how Eik Island harbor is going to be transformed into huge docks; they know all about the municipal engineer who goes around talking to people's wives, unable to pay his visits when the men are at home, but you, Arve Brunberg, since you work up in the Big Cross, you must know something about all this, and it is quiet as death when he says he doesn't know any more than they do. The bulkheads are so tight there that nothing leaks through, and there is a journalist from the local newspaper along on the ride, writing notes as they talk, and they become less talkative when they discover him, because nobody wants to be the first to take a stand. But Arve Brunberg sits with his face turned away, sensing that he is nearing the island. They dock, they're there. A herd of men go ashore on Eik Island, home from work with their lunch boxes in hand and the rain pelting them from the west. The ferry churns up the water as it takes on a few passengers, a municipal engineer from Ramvik and a fellow with him, but nobody speaks to him when he goes on board,

and standing there by the road in front of his house, as he and Arve Brunberg part company, Olver sees Anna-Marja's pale face behind the lace curtains. They agree to call each other, and go their separate ways—Olver to a woman who won't come out on the steps to meet him, and Arve to a locked door. He has to ring the doorbell at his own house. With the thickening clouds, the darkness falls more abruptly than usual and the lamps now being lighted in all the houses are pale yellow patches on the sheets of rain.

28

And the man writing sees Skogmann sitting inside the heavily paint-laden window frames of the postmaster's house, behind the thin, old lace curtains, at a table he can rest his elbows on, Skogmann, sitting there reading. The rain running down the panes makes rivulets in his face and ripples across his hands when he turns the pages. He is reading a book he borrowed on social-democratic perspectives and the section he is going through is on his own lifetime. But he can't manage to concentrate in his usual fashion, he reads a few pages and has to put the book down. The articles remain in his head with their suffocating language, alongside fragments and sentences from other years. And melodies he can't forget, while he stands watching the ferry crossing the fjord in the driving rain and fog, he wants to go down and see who's on it. "*Organization and processes and methods.*" "*See the sun's magnificent light and power.*" He puts on his poplin jacket and a thin coat over it made out of plastic. He gets warm quickly in this lightweight outfit. "*The international companies are restricted by national legislation.*" He shoves his hat down firmly on his head. Mephisto commands the ocean to recede so the green land appears. "*The eternal feminine gazes upon us.*" Askov. Christopher Bruun,

"*through its own organs the state must establish cooperation with the independent credit institutions.*" Skogmann goes out into the hallway where Henrietta's suitcases are waiting. "*As it must be our task to create a balance between the level of education and the demands of industry.*" "*The years of our youth are the best years of our lives.*" "*Will mature with diligence and with age.*"

Take along some money, in case he wants to buy something at the store. He peels back two layers of outer clothing and puts his wallet into the breast pocket of his shirt. He opens the door and goes out on the road. Here comes Karl Magnus Skogmann, lifting his feet high above the puddles. *The rosy mildness of evening. Stability and control.* He stops and looks at the two men going onboard the ferry when it docks. It is darker than it has been for a long time. Despite the wind, the island is closed in by the sky. A herd of workmen going ashore. The pupils from the middle school slinging their book bags and kicking up the gravel. He mulls over the theories of Christopher Bruun about how their lives ought to be. In the age of awkwardness, when physical beauty abandons them for a brief period, when the child's mirror of innocence is broken to pieces and the clear bell of their voices cracks, that is when they should be put to physical tasks which will give them the balance their later youth requires. He stands there watching them jangle past and suddenly sees that *this* is no longer relevant. He has no ideal for them to pattern their lives after anymore. What happens inside us happens on account of what happens around us. It happens despite our wishes and our hopes,

he stands and watches the people going home for dinner, the ferry putting out to sea again, the area around the landing, now empty. In a flash of imagination he builds the grand wharf that is proposed, envisions the big cranes swinging high above the storekeeper's house, the young men walking along the scaffolding high up on the ship's hull, raking in their first paychecks. Most people have no way of avoiding what will come. Those years of youth that according to Mr. Bruun ought to be the age of dreams, will be consumed in a frenzy of construction in the harbor area of Eik Island. And people walk home to dinner, a few dozen workers, a handful of school children. They come home to the housewives and mothers who take the lids off of steaming pots, or perhaps a hand, behind in its work, goes dancing around the edge of a tin can with an opener of shiny metal squeezed against the rim. Another pops the cork out of a bottle, and maybe some of them flick the skins off the potatoes as soon as they sit down at the table or a pair of lips blows on a large soup spoon. A comfortable weariness envelops them, they begin to talk about the report on the radio and what will happen to them. But down by the harbor Skogmann is standing alone, no one has dinner waiting for him. And his appetite has not left him yet.

29

But there is no dinner waiting for Olver Kretsen when he enters his little house either. Anna-Marja rushes over to him with the tale of what she should not have done. She didn't *want* to do this to him. He asks her to put the plates on the table.

He hurls himself into potato preparation, washing and scrubbing them, and is not visibly affected by anything. She tells him about the two men who came to see her when she was at the school at work. He keeps repeating at regular intervals: "It makes no difference, Anna-Marja, it doesn't mean a thing." But she doesn't believe him, thinks he must be keeping something from her because he doesn't think her nerves can take hearing the truth. She may have caused him a huge economic loss. "What is wrong with her?" he is thinking. His arms are tired and he gets out the newspaper when he has put the potatoes on to boil. He wonders what time would be appropriate to go over to Brunberg's, he must let Anna-Marja know that he has to go over there and dreads having to tell her. And he hears her say that he must know about this, since he runs around all over the Big Cross, must have an idea what they are planning over there. He knows nothing, but she doesn't want to listen to him. "She is just asking me to get rough with her," he thinks, "but I just can't do it. What good would it do?" She must want him to pound the table with his fist and tell her to shut up, but he would never do that! She changes the topic to keep the conversation going and begins to talk about Marianna.

"I wonder if Marianna is well today."

"I saw her at the cafe this morning."

"I don't think things are going too well for her."

"There is nothing seriously wrong with her."

"How are you supposed to know if an illness is serious or not?"

"I go by what she tells me herself."

"She doesn't take care of herself until it's too late."

"Not much we can do about it."

"But in any event, her first commitment should be to her job."

"I have no reason to believe they are unhappy with her at the cafe."

"When you have a job you've got to see that you do it."

"I've never heard anyone imply that Marianna wasn't doing a good job."

"But she could at least call me up. She knows that I'm worried about her."

"Since there's nothing wrong, it probably doesn't occur to her to call."

He buries his head behind the pages of the newspaper. She is sitting at the kitchen table attempting to straighten the knives and forks. His stomach is aching with hunger, but he doesn't dare mention it. He is

in the middle of an article about the district economy when he gets a strange feeling that something has happened in the room. He turns around and finds himself for the first time looking directly into Anna-Marja's blank gaze. She is sitting at the table banging harder and harder with the blunt end of a knife against the table cloth; she is no longer in the room, and she is whispering in a voice far away, while she bangs the knife handle into the table with every word: "You—don't—listen—to—what—I—say—to—you! You don't listen to what I say to you!! Youdon'tlistentowhatIsaytoyou!!! YOU DON'T LISTEN TO WHAT I SAY TO YOU,"

and he jumps up. The knife handle hits the table like a jack hammer and with every stroke her body moves more and more: her head, her shoulders, back and forth, larger and larger movements, louder and louder a scream emerges from the depths and fills the entire room: "You don't listen!" Thunk, thunk, thunk, she drops the knife and pounds with her fists against the thin table and after every word she screams, a sob follows, incomplete, a reverberation from tears she has suppressed for a long time, and her sobs become small screams, she gasps for breath "DON'T LISTEN!" Her body is losing its resistance, the loud scream is pressing its way out between her clenched teeth, and there it comes, long and loud, she throws herself down across the table and it comes in long bursts with choked words and parts of words in between.

He has planted his hands firmly on her shoulders now and is trying to calm her down, but she doesn't notice him, it appears. He speaks to her: "Anna-Marja," he says in a gentle voice he has never used before, but he cannot reach her, she throws her head against the oilcloth-covered table and screams and screams, and her crying has no end. The two boys have come in and are standing by the door to the little entryway, standing almost at attention, rain dripping from their clothes. Anna-Marja lies draped across the kitchen table, crying, her body tossing occasionally from side to side, crying away. He says to the children: "Take off your boots. Mother is sick." They just stand there looking at him with dark eyes. Olver: "Take them off and come over here." He thinks they may as well see her like this, so nothing will catch them unprepared later on. They slip out into the entryway and take off their boots, then come across the floor over to the stove where their half-cooked dinner sits. He tells them that they should go into the living room and play the record player for a while and they obey, closing the door carefully behind them. He is left standing in the middle of the floor, listening to her sobbing, now almost inaudible, now louder again. He doesn't know what to say to her. From time to time a plea bursts out: "Help me, Olver." He says "I'm right here by you." And he tries to do what she says when she asks him to hold her tight, because she doesn't know what she might try to do.

"Maybe you ought to lie down, Anna-Marja." He pulls her up from the chair and she goes along with him. He gets her up to the bedroom and she buries herself in the bedclothes, as if she were searching for something in them. He stands over her until she mumbles: "Leave me alone." He goes out of the room, blows out the lamp and closes the door behind him. Downstairs he dials the number for the emergency health services in Ramvik to get them to send someone over. But no one can come. The doctors' small launch can't be put into the water in this weather and if one of them takes the ferry over to Eik Island, they won't be able to get to Ramvik again until the next day. They promise to send some tablets that will calm her down, and

the whole time he is talking he hears sounds from her coming down through the floor of the loft. He doesn't dare leave her there. He calls Skogmann to have him fetch the medicine when the ferry arrives, but there is no answer. From the living room he hears the record player, from the loft Anna-Marja. Olver Kretsen calls the boys and gives them a piece of bread. As the knife slices through the bread he thinks: "I can't manage without her . . ."

30

In the guestroom at the teacher's house it is almost totally dark now; Henrietta Brunberg opens her eyes and her whole body aches. There beneath the heavy roof beams she can barely even move. Outside the window nature is doing its thing, and down on the first floor the record player is droning. Arve is home from work. When she turns over on her side to think about what to do, she feels a sharp pain in her chest that reminds her that her body is no longer twenty. But she gets up, goes to the bathroom to put herself back together, the whites of her eyes have turned red in the mirror, the bluish gray sacks still hang there beneath them. She fills the bathtub with water, although this will alert the man down there that she has gotten up. But she can't stay up there all evening. Sitting in the tub the warmth returns to her body, her brain starts working again, she thinks: "I have to decide. I have to decide fast,"

it's good to get clean. She washes her hair too, because it's short and will dry quickly. Lathers her scalp and thinks that it would have been nice to have a concrete complaint against him, so that she could say: "That and that and that." But at the same time she is thinking that she doesn't need any more assurance than she has; she has enough to base her decision on. She gets up. "As soon as I'm rested, I'll do it. I have the whole weekend to talk to him." One of the two men down there is coming up the stairs. She stands in the tub waiting, makes no attempt to cover herself up. Arve sticks his head in the door and looks at her: "Shall I make something to eat? What would you like?"

"Would you please go out until I am dressed?"

"Good heavens! Henrietta Brunberg has gotten shy."

"I'm not getting paid to stand here and have you stare at me."

When he doesn't move, she pulls the door shut from in front of his nose and locks it. She gets dressed quickly, goes downstairs, thinking: "Now I can do it, if I want,"

and their friend has cleared away the mess from the morning and entered into a new phase. All his movements are slow and rounded. He tries to maintain control and succeeds, Arve has slumped down into a chair, the friend of the family comes in with some drinks he has made: "Now we'll drink this, and we'll talk." Careful now. He hands each of them a glass. Henrietta suddenly remembers her daughter whom she hasn't seen for several days. Where is Liv?

"She is up at a friend's house. I told her there was a war going on at home."

"How long can that keep up? She must need some clothes at least."

"She'll probably come home later this evening."

The strong drink makes Henrietta light-headed and more impatient. Waves of heat are passing through her body. This spacious house, with all the wind outside it, is a prison she can suffocate in. She looks at the clock and realizes that she can make the six-thirty ferry to Ramvik if she hurries. She pours down her drink, gets to her feet and says:

"I have to make the ferry."

She has to hurry, her bags are still down at Skogmann's. She runs around quickly collecting her personal effects in a handbag and gets on her outer garments. They don't say anything more to her. Not until she is outside and Arve comes out on the steps and calls after her. Twenty meters away she barely pauses to hear:

"Are you coming back or aren't you?"

"I'll let you know tomorrow."

And she has to hurry off, otherwise she will turn around and go back.

the man writing drives her away, through the darkness, the rain, and the wind that sweeps along the west coast of Norway across Eik Island, Land Island and Vind Island, past the vacant area beneath a leafless birch tree by the road, down to the Eik Island docks. That is where Karl Magnus Skogmann was standing. Now he has gone home. Yesterday at the same time he was inviting a woman to come home with him, when he saw her standing on the dock, waiting. She has talked to him and brought him out of balance. And when he loses his balance, he gets tired, because he is an old postmaster who has spent the greater part of his life coming to terms with his ideals, but when he tried to talk to Henrietta the previous evening the words just stopped before they reached his lips,

where does he intend to go from here? He looks around in his little, illuminated box, perched there close by the blue-black current of the Eik Island Sound. The lights over on the other side of the fjord are lost in the drifting fog. He sits waiting. The telephone rings and it is Olver asking him to fetch some medicine for Anna-Marja. While he is standing there talking about what is wrong, someone knocks on the outer door. He has to hang up,

and there comes Henrietta Brunberg right into the room. Rain is dripping off her and she is blinded by the light so he can hope that she won't notice that his face undergoes a change.

"I have to go. My bags."

THE FERRY CROSSING

"Are you leaving for good?"

"There's no way I can know that yet."

He is glad that he has an errand. "I'll go with you down to the dock. I have to pick up some medicine for Kretsen." He hurries to get his two thin coats on.

"So, there are going to be some changes around here," he says, walking beside her as they near the docks and the storage shed. "Pretty soon there may not be anything here to come back to,"

he puts the suitcases down by the shed, the ferry is almost in. He looks at her face in the light from the floodlights above the ferry ramp. She takes his hand. "Farewell, Skogmann. Go on home, now. I don't want you to stand here and wait with me."

He doesn't protest.

But up on the road beneath a birch tree there, he turns around. She can't see him. He watches her go onboard. The man writing reminds Karl Magnus Skogmann about his errand. He goes back down and takes a package from one of the crewmen who has brought it ashore.

Part two

31

He is sitting at a cafe in the mountains outside of Molde, writing while darkness falls. He is sitting in the corner by the window, watching the car lights pass by on the road. People heading for their cabins even at this gray time of year, semi-trucks going to Hustad and Bud, Eide and Vevang. In the cafe a jukebox is grinding away, anyone may select the music. Just push the button you want and you get the music of your choice. That's all there is to it.

There is a jukebox in the corner of the Bus Station Cafe in Ramvik. There are not many people in the cafe, but the jukebox is playing. There is a waitress behind the counter, looking out into the serving area. She knows all the records by heart. She's not the one who selects the music, but she has to be there in the cafe and do the job she's been hired to do.

Every time she hears a vehicle outside she runs to the window. It is just past six-thirty. Over the loud speakers in the smoking area she hears the evening news from Oslo. They mention the municipality of Ramvik on the broadcast from Oslo. She doesn't catch what they say about it. She ought to have listened more closely, but she must constantly run to the window and see what kind of vehicles are driving by. Finally the one she has been waiting for arrives: the bus from Molde, lurching through the puddles on the street outside, with mud and grime on its sides and rain sparkling beneath its headlights. She calls to the kitchen crew that she is going out for a moment, throws on her raincoat, runs down the stairs, around the building, and over to the station office and waiting room where the bus is parked, letting the passengers out through two doors. The driver gets out last. She knows him. He goes to the baggage compartment beneath the bus and takes out a stack of newspapers tied with string: "Here are your newspapers, Metta, but they got a little wet."

"Do you want one today?" she asks him. "Want to see what's in it this time?"

"I bought one last time, that ought to hold me," he says.

"Did you think it was such a waste of time reading it?"

"Yes, if they think they can start a revolution in Norway!"

"Well, why not?"

"It would never work!"

"Nobody wants to change anything in this country. We are all too well off."

She has to leave: "We can talk more about it this evening."

"No! This evening we're having a party. Tell Marianna that the table is reserved for eight-thirty."

"You'll have to tell her yourself, she's not at work now."

"Oh, she isn't? What time are you coming tonight?"

"When I'm done here. You can expect me a little before ten."

She goes back up to the cafe and lays the pile of newspapers in a cabinet where the waitresses keep their belongings. Back at the counter she begins thinking about the help she is giving Marianna Kretsen. She's the one carrying the ball because Marianna wouldn't have had the initiative on her own. She has decided that no one should be involved except the ones who *have* to be. She takes responsibility on herself and never forces anyone to share it with her.

"Just a second. I'll check to see if we have more rolls in the kitchen."

"What are you thinking about so hard, Metta?"

The girl who has been in charge of dinner is standing next to her and wants to talk about her own problems now, because Metta always listens. Even if she doesn't always know what she should answer, people need someone to talk to who will just sit there and listen. "You know my son, the one in high school who can't do math. Well, I was thinking that you, Metta, since you certainly have studied math, that maybe you could give him a few tips . . ."

Metta asks: "What were they saying on the radio about Ramvik? And Eik Island?"

"Oh, something about shipbuilding. I didn't think it was important."

"It sounded a little bit strange."

"It's nothing for us to be concerned about. *You* don't even come from here."

"Well, in any case, I'm here right now."

She *was* there now, on that wind-blown coast, near the end of October, three quarters of an hour from Molde, in an almost empty cafe, along with a widow who had been the cafe cook since her husband died. She was there at that moment, Metta Nilsen, and she had to think and act as if she would be there forever, otherwise it would be intolerable.

"What is wrong with Marianna these days?"

"Nothing special, as far as I know."

"She has been so strange lately."

"Probably some kind of a mess with Hans."

"That's easy to imagine. He is not your most reliable person, I would guess."

"What do you know about *that?*"

"He was sitting here at the cafe talking about Marianna one evening. And the things he said he would never have said about someone he cared for."

The woman speaking walks over to the window and looks out.

Metta Nilsen has gotten help she wasn't expecting.

She takes a knife and goes into the little room where her newspapers are. She cuts the string off and looks at the headlines. The headlines in a monthly newspaper which professes to be about war: the war between the classes in society. Big words. Empty words? *Workers of the world, unite! EEC—an imperialist threat to Norway.* This is what she has elected to tell

the people in Ramvik, the ones who live in aging wooden houses all the way up to the City Hall and the cafe building, or in the two municipal apartment houses put up right after the war. Or in the new apartment complexes south and east of the municipal center, on the hills there. These are the people she is going to talk to about socialism. When she went to the Folk High School, before she got involved in this, she could say whatever she pleased about life and nobody held her responsible. Now she has a responsibility. The people who run the organization she is in have a right to expect that she will sell her thirty copies of the newspaper. If she had had the people who run the organization here, she would have asked them about Marianna. But here she has no one to ask. Here she's the boss,

no one to ask? There are four or five members, even here. But they are all younger than she is. Two pimply high school pupils, a bookworm of an inventory clerk from an electrical supplies company, who knows a lot, but never says a word, so punctual that he will be early at his own funeral, but so slow to speak that he never accomplishes anything. How can they help her? Before she hurries back into the serving area, she decides to call in the Young Socialists. She needs their opinion. She might have been able to get them together this evening already. But then she would have to cancel the date with Marianna.

In her next break she tears a piece off her pad for taking orders, thinks for a moment, and writes: "A sympathizer has personal problems. We need to discuss what we can do." She puts the note in her apron pocket and keeps it there until the daily newspaper boy comes in a half hour later with the day's edition of *Dagbladet*. He sits down at a table and has a cup of coffee. Metta looks at him, he smiles at her, but she can't bring herself to smile back at him, because she's standing there sizing him up: "What advice can *he* give me? What can *he* understand of what goes on inside a girl who is going to have a baby she doesn't want?" No matter. She is forced to listen, to him. To them. She goes over to him and gives him the note: "Eleven tomorrow morning. Same place as last time." And she goes back to her place by the counter. Outside she hears the bus to Molde, vibrating impatiently as it waits for the ferry to Eik Island, which is late, and that starts the whole thing: the bus arrives late in Molde, the ferry from Molde to Vestnes doesn't wait, and neither does the bus from Molde to Åndalsnes, so the people who want connections from that town in this weather don't have many alternatives. But the ferry is nearing Ramvik,

32

and up in the loft room in the dark, beneath the rain that drums on Olver Kretsen's tile roof, inside the walls where the water is running down from the troughs into the downspouts, Anna-Marja Kretsen is lying in bed emitting her great cry in small portions. The light from the hallway in the loft comes through the keyhole, and she hears Olver talking to the children in the kitchen below. She hears him turn on the radio and that the news is on, but she isn't sure whether it's seven o'clock or ten. Little by little the knots begin to untie themselves, she gets calmer, she can stretch out her coiled up body, open her eyes so she doesn't have to see the image she sees, a sledge hammer falling rapidly toward a skull, blood, and Marianna assaulted and left lying in a ditch. Their youngest boy, where is he, has he gone to sea, will she never see him again? She strains to hear his voice down in the kitchen. She doesn't dare go down. And Olver with his face behind the newspaper doesn't even turn around when she speaks to him, because she doesn't exist for him any longer. This island that she can never get away from, the trips to the store where she begins sweating as she searches for her shopping list: where did I put that list! The people from the island stand around and watch her. While the storekeeper gets the various items she is struck with panic, the fear that she may not have enough money with her. Arguing with herself: it makes no difference in the world, you can go home and get more money or say that Olver will come and pay when he comes home from work. All the same she stands there stiff with anxiety, watching the storekeeper adding, first by hand, then on his machine, how will this end, Anna-Marja Kretsen? It's far from certain that you'll be able to account for yourself, far from certain that you will measure up, you can't even manage your own house any longer, even though you don't have much else to occupy you. And you think you would be able to hold down a job in a public place? That is sheer madness. Now people are going to find out that you are sick and they will look at you on the road, from the back and from the side, convinced that you may have another breakdown at any time. Anna-Marja Kretsen thinks, between the thoughts she has no control over, "I want to get away, away, get admitted to a hospital at least for a short while, so I don't have to stay here and look at the same old things, a hospital where there are other people like me, where I don't have anything to be ashamed of. Because here a person has to be ashamed of not fulfilling his obligations when there is apparently nothing keeping him from it." Anna-Marja Kretsen has a husband and children to take care of, a husband who is good to her. She has enough money to keep the house up, enough so that Olver can eat well when he comes home from work. But she can't manage. She is afraid of people when she's out, of herself when she's at home. She has kept her illness hidden from the one who cares about her most, because she doesn't want to bother him. But now. When she can't manage any longer, how will it be for him now,

the telephone is ringing down there. She tries to stop her heart so she can hear what he is saying, whether he is talking about her, please no, he mustn't! But she can't catch it, although the house is far from soundproof. She hears him mention Marianna's name. Surely there can't be anything wrong with Marianna! "There *is* something wrong with Marianna! I knew it. That's why I lost control of things today."

She gets up, stumbles, barefoot, across the floor, toward the keyhole where the light is coming from, gets the door open, walks over to the stairs. He is still standing holding the telephone, talking. She stops halfway down the stairs and stares at him. It must not be sinking in, whatever he is hearing about Marianna! "Olver! What is it? What has happened to Marianna?"

he turns and waves her away, finishes the conversation, hangs up, comes over to her. "There wasn't anything wrong. Just someone who wanted to know if she was here, but I gave him the telephone number of her landlords and told him to call there." "What do they want with her? What do they need to get hold of Marianna for? There must be something going on, I wouldn't just get sick without a reason." "Go up and lie down, Anna-Marja, get some rest and everything will be fine,"

he follows her up the stairs. "Lie down now, I have some medicine for you." They hear someone talking to the boys down in the kitchen. "That's Skogmann now!" and Olver Kretsen hurries downstairs. She gets back under the comforter and puts out the light, squeezes the edge of the bed with her hand as she moans softly.

Karl Magnus Skogmann, the deposed postmaster. He comes in through the entryway on the back side of Olver Kretsen's house. He stands there in the door opening with his two coats on and the medicine that is going to make Anna-Marja calm. The two boys are sitting at the table with comic books and a reader. Olver is busy making their dinner. He is glad that Skogmann is there. Skogmann in the doorway, waiting for a "Please come in" before he steps inside, sits down on a chair, removes his wet hat carefully and puts it down on the floor beside him: "The medicine came, but the doctor didn't."

33

And neither did anyone come along to stop Hans Kristiansson, as he drove around on the country roads on the Romsdal Peninsula hour after hour. He felt his ability to breathe coming back as the needle on the speedometer climbed higher. But breathing difficulties tend to recur, and a half tank of gasoline doesn't last forever. He has been far out in the countryside, looking for an old friend who might listen, if someone asked him. But the friend went to Sweden several months ago. On the way back Hans Kristiansson stopped at a cafe situated in the mountains outside of Molde, and now he goes in to spend his last few crowns on coffee. He doesn't have enough for cigarettes,

and it's just like when your matches are wet and useless, and someone hands the last inch of his cigarette to you so that *you* can light yours from the remaining glow and not put it out until he, in turn, has lighted a new one from yours,

just like that, in there in the dim cafe, a man sits writing, putting sentences in a notebook. He gets the feeling that someone is standing behind him, watching him. Right afterwards a young man, no more than twenty, comes over to him and bums a cigarette. He gives it to him and continues writing the story of Hans Kristiansson, who goes over to a table in the cafe

and asks to bum a cigarette from a man who sits there writing, around seven in the evening in a cafe in the mountains. The guy barely looks at him, just says "Be my guest." Hans goes back to his table. He has to go back to Molde. Just as he has put on his jacket and is heading for the door, the guy with the notebook comes running after him and says: "Are you going to Molde? Could I get a ride with you?"

They are sitting in the car on the way to Molde and Hans asks:
"What were you making notes about? It looked peculiar."
"I'm writing a book."
"Oh, really, what's it about?"
"That's not such an easy question. About people, I guess."
"What kind of people?"
"I can't really say, until the book is finished."

"That's a good answer," says Hans. "So you go up to the mountains to get an overview or whatever."

"I suppose."

"And you get a fantastic overview in this fog, don't you!"

"The darkness helps, too."

"It will get darker than this," says Hans. He steps on the accelerator for the last stretch toward the city. "Where do you want to get out, by the way?"

The man hasn't thought about this, but he is staying at Romsdalsheimen. He may actually be flying back to Oslo this evening.

But in this weather the planes can't get off the ground.

"I know what you should do. You ought to go and say hello to a colleague of yours who lives here in town. His name is Hans Kristiansson and he writes romantic novels."

"I've never heard of him."

"That doesn't surprise me. He writes under a pseudonym. But, anyway, he does write. And he is always interested in talking with authors."

"Oh, really. . ."

"Is the stuff you write exciting?"

"Well, yes and no."

"Hans Kristiansson, now there's a fellow who writes exciting books. I'll drive you over to his place. Say hello from me. You won't regret having made his acquaintance."

Way out on Bjørsetlia they stop. Hans stops a little way from his parents' house and points: "You see over there?"

"He has a fancy house, that Mr. Kristiansson."

"Earns a lot from his books, you know. Just ring the doorbell. I have to rush off. I have an appointment,"

in the rearview mirror Hans sees the fellow standing a bit confused at the side of the road before he starts walking over to the house where his father lives. Hans grins and drives on. Over Moldeli Road and Langmyr Road down to Fuglset and to Øverland, to the low apartment buildings down there. Which entrance is hers? It is dark now, and his watch has stopped. He goes from door to door, looking closely at the names by the doorbells. Finally he finds hers, just when he was thinking she might have moved. Of course, she hasn't moved. He doesn't have time to make plans, he'll just have to get to her any way he can. He rings the bell. A little wait, then she appears in the doorway, Elina, the secretary of his father.

34

But through the door of the Bus Station Cafe in Ramvik walks a dripping wet woman and puts her gloves and purse on a table. At the counter she asks the waitress if there isn't a bus to Molde later that evening. There is, and what's more, there is one leaving now.

"I know that, but I would like to wait a bit."

It is Henrietta Brunberg, ordering coffee.

She looks as if she were on a journey.

She sits at the table and looks at the waitress traipsing back and forth behind the counter. After a while she asks if she may use the telephone to call a couple, also teachers, whom she and Arve often visit. But it must be an inconvenient time for them, since they don't invite her over. Time passes, and no one is expecting her in Molde either. There is no one waiting for her anywhere, except the man she has left. Is it his fault that nobody is waiting? He always wanted it to be just the two of them. Now that it is no longer the two of them, there is nobody. She smokes cigarettes like a lady whose lover has left her in the movies. She is wet, sleepy and half frozen. She buys more cigarettes at the counter, because she doesn't like sitting there without a good reason. She asks at the counter if there are always so few people in the cafe,

not always. But this evening there is a dance at the hotel. Those who are going out will all be going there. Reserved tables only. Henrietta Brunberg asks to use the telephone. She calls and asks if there is still a table available. And a room. A room for two and a table for two.

"Then we'll be seeing each other over at the hotel," says the waitress and takes the money for the phone call. "I am going over there, too, when my shift is over." Henrietta Brunberg walks through the rain the few hundred meters over to the old hotel building from back in the golden days when Ramvik was a big fishing town and people came in boats to do business. She gets the keys and unlocks the door to a room with a large bed in the middle, and a newly remodelled bathroom with white towels that beg to have blood on them. A large, old mirror hangs on the inside of the closet door that she leaves standing open. The window looks out on a bleak inner courtyard and a low building on the other side sporting its own row of windows and a group of people behind them in a living room. She is about to draw the curtains, but changes her mind. They can just as well spy on her, for all she cares, in fact, she hopes they *will*. Then, out of the suitcase she pulls a wrinkled party dress to change into, and goes into the bathroom anyway and shuts the door behind her.

The bed is much too large for her alone. It is as though she is lying on the edge of a precipice while she rests before going downstairs. She doesn't dare lie comfortably, because she is afraid that the dress will get even worse and she can't bear to take it off again. She dreads going down there like she is, wet, disheveled, clammy, pale from lack of sleep, and with a headache from drinking that morning. Should she order something from room service first, so she can get some warmth in her veins before she goes down, maybe a glass of port? But a woman alone, especially one who is a teacher in the grade school on Eik Island, can't very well lie in bed in a hotel room in Ramvik and drink port. No, that wouldn't do, and neither can she go down to the restaurant alone. There will surely be someone she knows there to latch onto and ask to share her table with her. Would anybody be bold enough to turn down the offer of sharing her table? She doesn't look that terrible, does she? She looks down at herself and feels ashamed. Is this anything to offer to an acquaintance at a restaurant. Hasn't she sold enough of her soul as it is? She has to go down there, have a drink, dance with whomever she pleases, and leave the restaurant quietly and without being noticed when she has drunk enough that she can sleep.

Elina, standing there in the doorway like a great, half-opened eye, holding her bathrobe closed at the neck. She whispers: "Is it you? Wait a minute." "No," says Hans. He opens the door and goes inside. "Get back under the comforter, I don't want you to get up." There is a little living room with a kitchen area in one corner and a door into the bedroom. She walks hesitantly in and sits down on the bed, just sits and looks at him in her white bathrobe which she holds tightly together at the neck. Can't that damned woman wear anything but white and black? "Do you have something I can make a sandwich out of. Never mind, I'll find it myself. Lie down again, I said." He finds himself some food in the refrigerator. He comes into her bedroom. She sits upright in the bed while he chews, with the comforter pulled up all around her—a white one, of course—and he tells her about how he

walks into this used-car place and gets himself a car, so he can go racing around on the backroads. Her fear begins to lose its grip on her. She mumbles: "That car dealer must be the only person in town who doesn't know what your father thinks of you." He tells about the man who was sitting in the cafe writing in a huge notebook, "so big that he had to put it on the back seat in order to have room to sit in the front when we drove down to town, and I sent him over to my parents' house. He went right over and rang the doorbell, I was sitting in the car waiting, they didn't see me, father came out and opened the door, and the guy just stood there crestfallen, no idea what to say and when he came back, all confused, I started the car and drove away like a bat out of Hades, and straight over here,"

to a little apartment on Øverlandsvegen,

the man writing, left standing on the road looking around, not knowing where he ought to go, thinks "an apartment house on Øverlandsvegen"

where Hans Kristiansson sits explaining that he has been giving some thought to marrying Marianna, because she is one hell of a nice girl. ("You never said that before.") He has always said that! He wants to do things right for her. He'll show those guys who think he's just full of the devil, he'll show them all right,

he moves over to the bed and sits down by her while he is talking, he talks without stopping, talks to her and says: "Besides, you are the only person who understands me in this town, but you'll prove to be right, I'll show them who can get things done around here." While he is talking he puts his hand under the comforter and runs it up along her body. She jumps, but doesn't say anything, so he takes that as a sign of approval, reaches up and turns off the light. "What do you think you're doing! Hans!" he hears her say in the darkness, but he is so sure that he is man enough for anyone, "Stop it! You know I'm a respectable person." She says she won't allow this. Hans: "What are you talking about? It never occurred to me." He wriggles down next to her, still going on about how she is the only person who cares about him. She tries to take his hands off her, but she gives in, naturally she gives in, because he is just bold enough, and he knows it. He runs his hand along her hips to get her bathrobe out of the way and holds her tight, but without being brutal. She says: "Hans!" "Yes, I'm right here," and she goes limp, because she doesn't know what might happen otherwise. She is not willing, just passive, trembling as she lies there, and it is irrelevant to him whether she is willing or not. He pushes his way inside her; she is not a virgin as he had imagined, and when he is inside, he tries to take it easy and wait for her. He thinks: "I'm not going to let go until I know she's with me." He speaks softly and quickly: "This is good, Elina, this is good for us. This is so good, because I feel that you trust me, I really feel it now. This is good for us. I want to be good to you." And his body rests lightly against hers. She whispers: "We shouldn't . . ." but he supports himself on his elbows, so light above her, until he feels that she can't hold back, that there is something in her that is stronger than the unwillingness to go along with him. Her hips rise toward him, she doesn't want to, but she is doing it all the same, and he himself is hardly excited at all. He meets her: "Yes, yes, yes," and her hands fall to embrace his body, squeeze him (slow, now! she's almost there!) and he just follows along, lightly above her. She's the one in a hurry now, he can keep this up as long as need be, what a man! The bed begins to creak, but she no longer hears it, he thinks, peak after peak and she screams—he feels almost nothing, but she is screaming with her mouth wide open. Until it turns into sobbing, her body begins to tremble and she turns away from him and cries.

    He sits up and swings his feet out over the side of the bed. In the darkness he pulls on his pants and goes over to the window and the lights beyond, Bolsønes Shipyard, the beach leading out to the airport. When he turns again, he catches a glimpse of her face. She is lying completely still, the crying is over, he knows that she is lying there looking at him. He says that he has to leave soon, and what is she supposed to reply? But first he turns the ceiling light on and asks her to get up. She does what he asks, she gets up and goes to the sink and fills the coffee pot with water.

At that moment Henrietta Brunberg gets up, in her room at the Ramvik Hotel, to go downstairs to the party and the people. She catches sight of the ring on her hand, when she looks in the mirror, thinks for a second, takes it off and tosses it into a drawer. She is excited and nervous, thinking that now she is going to run around here playing the part of an available woman, pretending that no one owns her. She will be a woman on the same footing with the others there, constructing her evening on the same male ulterior motives as they will. In the lobby she views herself in a large mirror, her long dress fits her well, the color has returned to her cheeks, she feels that she looks good. This country is so small that the waiter knows who she is, "Good evening, Mrs. Brunberg." Her table is on the edge of the salon, next to the orchestra which is still playing muted dinner music. She gets a menu and wine list and the waiter asks, "And the other person?" She looks at the empty chair, could just as well tell the truth, say that no one is coming, but instead she informs him that, "My husband will be coming from Molde sometime this evening, I don't know when he will arrive. Please let me know if he telephones."

people come in through the doors, a strange mixture of forgotten old-timers and newly-arrived doctors and municipal administrators, along with the youth of Ramvik who have been away from home and learned to go to restaurants, sailors home from the sea and students who have ditched their studies to do substitute teaching at the Ramvik High School. They fill up the tables, and the music begins to get lively. Henrietta watches them while she pretends to read the wine list, and there comes the daughter of Olver Kretsen from Eik Island, Marianna, with her hair done up on top of her head and wearing a much too summery dress, and sits down at one of the tables.

35

But over on Eik Island Olver Kretsen and Karl Magnus Skogmann are using this time to work their way into a serious conversation. Because you don't just jump right in when you have something serious to discuss. The boys at the table soon leave and go to bed quietly. The older one talks about their mother as they climb the stairs: "Tomorrow we'll figure out something, you and I." Arve Brunberg calls on the telephone to find out if Olver Kretsen will be coming over soon. Olver tells him briefly what the situation is. When he is sure that the boys won't be coming down again, he goes to the cabinet. In there, far back behind the turpentine and paint cans, is the remainder of a bottle of liquor. "This is all I have to offer you. Anna-Marja has been the one who does the serving up to now." He pours small shots into large glasses. Skogmann drinks reverently. They talk about the changes that are to come to Eik Island and who will benefit from them. And Olver Kretsen sits there,

in his house beneath the newly tiled roof, and talks his way along from back in the days when he first came to Ramvik. That was back when they thought that industry would grow and flourish and put an end to the old society by itself. An era when the men who moved from one construction job to another had no desire to putter around with small-scale farming and fishing. Get rid of the old ways, and the future will appear automatically.

An era when they were counting on change.

An era when he thought he would go so far that he would one day be helping to shape the future of those two little tykes creeping up the stairs. And now: He sits in the bottom of a colossus that was erected over there in Ramvik, and knows nothing about what goes on on the upper floors. They call him when a light bulb burns out, or a desk drawer gets stuck. But he never finds out what is in the drawer once he has gotten it open; he takes the elevator down to the basement again and sits there, waiting.

There was the time when he went to the municipal engineer and wanted to get hold of a couple of copies of the proposed master plan for Ramvik. He was interested, he said, in finding out how things would look, even though he didn't have anything official to do with it. The municipal engineer looked at him and said it wasn't easy, no, it was no simple matter, but he would ask the mayor the next time he saw him. "After two months I went back and asked again. It must have been difficult indeed. The executive committee had decided that only members of the city council would be allowed to look at it initially, and they had taken an oath of confidentiality, of course, because it would not be to the advantage of the municipality to launch a public debate before the planning stage was properly concluded, since there are so many conflicting factions, so that . . . But it was never my intention to start a debate! I just wanted to stay informed. 'That is commendable,' they said, 'but as a matter of principle such plans are never placed in the hands of, well, of unauthorized persons, because imagine what would happen if the landowners began causing trouble now, who would be served by that? The Conservatives, Kretsen, and with your political views you wouldn't be able to come up with anything the Conservatives would be happy with. We have had a Labor government in Ramvik for all the years since the war, but we are not completely secure, no, we're just not secure, and it wouldn't take much more than getting the property owners riled up over the master plan, and that would be that. And furthermore, it isn't a plan, but a proposal,'"

and instead of being allowed to see the master plan, Olver Kretsen, the assistant to the head custodian in the Big Cross, is invited to a dinner to celebrate the sixtieth anniversary of the Ramvik Labor Party. He was to bring Anna-Marja along, but she didn't want to go, and so he was placed at the end of the table next to a woman who had made the coffee for all the meetings of the party's steering committee since the war. Aside from the two of them, there are only fancy people at the celebration. It starts according to etiquette with an appetizer and speeches here and there at all the proper pauses during the meal, continues with the doors to the grand ballroom in the Big Cross being opened to the regular party members as well, since only the upper echelon is invited to the dinner, but afterwards there is to be coffee and after-dinner speeches and workers' songs and dancing,

oh, how they sing! Olver Kretsen sits and looks down at his coffee cup, but glances over at the smaller tables once in a while. They sing and sing, don't bother to open the song books, they know them all by heart, sing so you can hear it throughout the Big Cross, and clap for the songs afterwards, in a festive mood. And after the singing: a speech by the General Secretary of the Labor Party, who has come all the way from Oslo to take part in this anniversary celebration, and they clap for him as he walks toward the podium, clap as though they will never stop, our general secretary, our general, Olver Kretsen's general for many years, now officially retired from the position, but still as active as ever in defending the ideals that the worker's movement . . . there he stands at the podium, the pitcher and the glass, the slanted platform for the manuscript, *him* with a manuscript?? in the ballroom in the new city hall (Congratulations on the magnificent building!) stroking his gray, no, white mane back away from his face and casting a glance around the room that tells his audience he has just come in out of the storm of life now raging outside. He fixes his gaze on the window in the west wall, this is late in the spring and the evening sun shines right in on him, but he won't allow himself to be blinded by it. He opens his mouth and the people assembled there know that now he is not just speaking to them, now he is speaking to the entire Norwegian nation. He is speaking about the grand foreign aid scheme for India and the people down there, a handshake from the Norwegian workers to their brothers across the globe. And the poverty and the need and the corruption and the illiteracy! He speaks at once flowingly and with sudden punctuation for impact. Something about it makes Olver Kretsen think about candle wax dripping, a duplicity in the voice being hurled against him that gives people a sense of both guilt and righteousness at the same time. Look at the backs around the little tables below the podium, straight, at-attention backs: *the labor movement, our boys on the floor.* The foreign aid program in Ceylon, an island off the coast of India (Olver Kretsen has to think about Eik Island), a handshake built on the labor movement's basic premise: solidarity. And our powerful neighbors, China and the Soviet Union, communism, the poison which spreads wherever need is great and people are unenlightened (unenlightened just like me, Olver Kretsen thinks), can we help to stop this poison in that huge country? And, via the connection with European brotherhood, the old fellow is back on Norwegian soil. We have elections coming up, and our foreign policy may not be top on the agenda, before we can turn our gaze outward, we must come to terms with our opponents here at home. But it must be stated clearly, that only through European co-operation, a community based on an equality with other democratic nations, can the Norwegian labor movement achieve its foremost goals, which in today's world are, number one (holding one finger aloft) limiting the power of the giant international corporations, and number two (second finger) insuring that we in this country will continue to live with democratic institutions, chosen by the people, and preserve our ideals in the face of the powers that threaten us, it was an anniversary address with substance. His voice rose toward the conclusion, it was no longer the man with the white hair speaking, but rather something speaking through him. His tie pin glittered like a star as he thrust his torso from side to side at the narrow podium, his water pitcher still untouched. The mayor of Ramvik sat next to the speaker, fooling with his portable tape recorder, he wanted to be sure to get these memorable words on tape. The secretary had gone over to domestic issues now, he was tackling the problem of poor government since that sly farmer from Trøndelag came to power, the decline in residential construction, the increase in prices, and the unjustified taxation of the working people: "Is this conservative administration doing anything about it? No, absolutely nothing! Should the Norwegian people resign themselves to such a government? No, absolutely not! Let us work together, comrades, for many more good years for the Ramvik Labor Party and a good election for the Norwegian labor movement. Applause. Applause. And what a man. The woman next to Olver turns to him with "What a man!" and Olver mumbles: "Yes, he is clever at speech making." The applause seems as though it will never end, even Olver Kretsen is sitting there slapping his palms against each other, without enthusiasm to be sure, but he is doing it,

and now he is sitting there, telling this to Karl Magnus Skogmann. He looks at his hands and perhaps he feels a tiny twinge of bad conscience because he is sitting there betraying one of his fellow party members to a moderate. He looks at the hands that have clapped for the General Secretary and screwed in new light bulbs at the Big Cross. He remembers the dance after the speech, Olver had no reason to be there, he had liked to dance before, but just couldn't get into it with these people. He sat in a corner and watched as people who had come to represent other divisions of the party from all over the county disappeared to a certain office along with one of the administrators, and they came back with a more radiant and venerable expression, like at a party at the youth center, and they invited each other's wives to dance, as is the custom in high society. The dance went on. The floor was strewn with white powder, the Ramvik Labor Party knows how to do things right. But the surface was as slick as ice, they whirled around, their feet slid easily, they danced doggedly, deliberately, they dipped their partners, swung them around, violently, and the dance went on, they played the old favorite melodies from those memorable years in the labor youth club before the war. Now it all came back to them. They had worked their way up, in politics and in the bread lines and now they were civil servants with municipal posts, it had taken the fifties and half of the sixties, but what does that matter, now their turn had come again. And in their midst sat Olver Kretsen, looking at his hands, just as he is now sitting in his own house with Karl Magnus Skogmann, the old postmaster, who is now recalling a little quotation from Christopher Bruun: "In the days of our youth we must dream the dreams that our manhood will come to fulfill." Could it have been the Big Cross the members of the Ramvik Labor Party once dreamed about?

And he thought about what he himself had been imagining recently: that some of the youth would come back to the island, young people who would make an effort to fix up the youth center, someone with guitars and accordions who could liven things up so that he didn't have to stand there, staring out across the Eik Island Sound. Maybe the population would increase again. But that would probably never happen. So they would just have to live with it, if things turned out some other way.

There is movement up in the loft and Olver hurries up there. Skogmann sits in the kitchen, waiting, while an alarm clock ticks away the minutes. He is not in a hurry about anything. But he is tired and his body aches, maybe it is the result of being up so late the night before. The telephone rings, Olver comes clunking down the stairs, answers it and speaks quickly. He comes into the kitchen and says: "Someone keeps calling, asking for Marianna." Skogmann: "I was the one who told her mother that Marianna ought to go to the Folk High School." Olver: "I was aware of that."

But he, Karl Magnus Skogmann, hasn't gone very often to the Bus Station Cafe since Marianna started working there. He doesn't like to see her there, wiping off tables and washing dirty dishes, that isn't what he envisioned for her. He can tell himself that it is just a transitional phase, but somehow the thought keeps popping up that there is something wrong with his ideals. Because the school he got her to travel all that distance to attend hasn't qualified her to do anything more than be a waitress at a cafe. It enters his mind again that his ideals are too old and no longer of any use. Not to mention another woman he knows, who is now in the process of leaving.

36

... But over at the teacher's house where Arve Brunberg lives on the northernmost point of Eik Island, the man writing lets the friend of the family come back, with a bottle that he has gone hopping over the hillocks to his mother's house to get. The water is dripping off him and the mud is up over the tops of his patent leather shoes, as he goes about singing and preparing a new round of drinks for Arve and himself. "I'm singin' in the rain," and he takes his seat, crosses his legs, starts his foot swinging and launches into a story about his longing and his sailor's heart. "You have become a cripple," he says to Arve, "from that sedentary office life you have gotten so used to. You ought to try to use your body once in a while, so you wouldn't have such a weakness for the girls either,"

"And if you hadn't been keeping house here all day long," says Arve stubbornly, "maybe I could have salvaged the evening. I had an appointment with Olver Kretsen for us to get together and discuss some of the things that are wrong on this island (maybe I know a little more than you think), and I intend to keep it, I intend to do something. You can sit there and think about Henrietta." He looks up a number in the telephone book and jots it down so as to have something to fiddle with, and dials with a trembling index finger, but Olver's wife has gotten sick, he has to sit down again: "I think all the women around here are nuts, they prevent anything from ever getting done."

He lets his gaze wander around the room and notices for the first time that everything he sees is the work of Henrietta's imagination. Those half-sick paintings she has hung up all around, the crazy colors of the curtains, the door sills, the lamp shades, he went along with it all, without protest. "Just do it however you like," he kept saying. Now he realizes that she has, out of pure malice, put together an environment for their life which doesn't harmonize, colors that clash completely, an overabundance of things they have no use for, this man who has always been a man of taste, never even opened his mouth to criticize her, just kept thinking: "It makes no difference to me, just let her go on until she realizes it on her own." Now he knows that if he had just spoken up, made some suggestions of his own, she would have been happy for them, and maybe things would have been easier then. ("She must be arriving to meet that lover of hers about now.") She wanted to respect and appreciate him, but he never showed her who he really was, and now he was gone, as far as she was concerned. He was invisible, a transparent container with nothing inside it, an empty space in thin air that arrived with the ferry from Ramvik every afternoon. He turns around and points: "You see that wall there, the one that divides Henrietta's desk area from the rest of the room?" Here stands the man who built it. God, how she nagged at me to build that wall. I said to her: 'What do you want a wall there for, nobody's going to make any noise here when you sit down to work at your desk. I can always manage to shut up and Liv can go upstairs.' Of course, she would have. Liv has always had her things up in her room and never been one to pester her mother all the time. But no, no that would never do. 'I have difficulty concentrating with you sitting there glowering at my back,' she said. 'I can just feel that hurt look of yours because I'm not sitting there keeping you company. I know that you are just waiting for me to get done, so we can sit there together again with nothing to talk about. You can't even read a book. You have to sit there clearing your throat, or putter around restlessly. I want to have a wall behind me, a little niche all my own. I have a lot to think about, that's part of my job as a teacher.'

And I gave in. Want a wall? O.K. A wall it will be! I never wanted to keep her from being independent, I never wanted to be difficult, I always gave her what she asked for (now she'll just have to see whether this other guy will, when she isn't all that exciting any more). So, no sooner said than done: I went to the Ramvik Lumber Supply to buy plywood panelling for that little piece of wall she wanted behind her back, it would only take a single evening to fix it up. She says that maybe it would be best if I hired someone to do it, but I really want to show her what I can do,

well, so I go in there and say I want six square meters of plywood paneling for my wife to sit behind. There they stand, these clerks who can't manage to bring in enough income to pay the rent without help from society, I know, I've got their files. They stand there and say that there is this kind of plywood paneling and that kind of plywood paneling, different thicknesses and types of wood, and it really ought to match what is already in my living room: what type is that? I am not familiar with the modern science of paneling, so they get out brochures and samples. I can't just stand there and say that I really don't have the faintest idea which type we have, so I point at one that looks familiar and say that's the one. Could I please have such and such an amount

THE FERRY CROSSING

of it put on the Eik Island ferry that afternoon. I carry the whole load of it up from the ferry landing to our house, and of course, it is the wrong type, and I can't ruin the appearance of the whole house, now can I? Henrietta laughs, right, she laughs and says: 'There's nothing to do but take it back and exchange it, Arve my boy.' I think: 'The hell I will,' and I carry it down to the basement and stack it there. That evening I get out the original architect's drawings and copy down the correct number for the paneling and ask Olver Kretsen to re-order it for me.

And so he is ready to put the wall up, and she is standing there over him while he kneels and measures the length of the paneling, (he has no tape measure, and has to use the one from her sewing box). She stands over him and says: "Shouldn't I go to the neighbor's and borrow a carpenter's square so you don't run the risk of sawing it crooked?" "NO!" she should definitely not do that, if he needs a square he can buy one, he eyeballs it over and over again and it turns out nearly straight. When he gets the trim on, it looks almost perfect, but before that he asks her to please leave the room while he puts on the finishing touches. He can't stand to have people breathing down his neck. He crouches over the fresh lumber, gets sap on his hands, sticky and impossible to get off again, feels the collar of his shirt getting wet with sweat, but he gets the job done as well as he can, hammers it in place, a hiding place for Henrietta, and goes off to bed. She was already there, in the darkness, when he crawled into bed: "I'm almost done." Henrietta: "How clever of you, Arve," and strokes his stomach with her hand. He knows what she wants, and he can't let her down. He goes after her with a saw and hammer, and for the first time he can't get it up, no matter how hard he presses himself against her and tries to conjure up images in his head that will set things straight, like an illustration of a couple making love in a book he once read (which made him tremble with excitement), that helps a little, but it's no use, and he turns his back to her, mumbling: "I don't think you really want to." She says: "Come on, Arve, this is no championship. It doesn't matter!" And he says: "I don't know what you're talking about." Then she tries to help him, but it is just no use, and he goes downstairs and sits there until she is asleep.

The next day she says that she has bought a new desk for the office ("which you built for me!"), and he replies that naturally she should have a new desk, now that they have spent the money to make the work area for her, and the desk arrives with six lockable drawers—for school compositions! But, of course, she has other things to hide there. Letters that come with no return address on them, Arve brings them home from the mailbox down by the storekeeper's, and she goes into her hiding place to read them. She is openly concealing things from him. The little alcove in the corner of the living room is a large recess inside her, which he is not allowed to enter. He doesn't say anything to her about this, and he feels that *that* was when all this started, this business he seems to be seeing the end of now.

He tries to get used to it. He tries to come up with interests of his own again. He starts reading journals and reports about the work he does. He even buys books. And he goes to the Ramvik library on the fourth floor of the Big Cross before the ferry leaves in the afternoon. But he doesn't know what book to check out because he doesn't have anything special in mind, just something or other to keep him busy. And just imagine how it must look to people at the Ramvik library when he just wanders around at random, when Arve Brunberg tries to walk quietly back and forth, glancing at the shelves and paging through books, and maybe he finds nothing or maybe he checks out ten books at once. But then he can't read them before they are due again, and he lugs a full briefcase back across the Eik Island Sound.

37

The man writing will soon be unable to think of anything but water. It is running off him, as he gropes his way along the side roads and dead end streets, trying to find the Romsdalsheimen Hotel where he is staying. He totally ignores the map on the wall in the stairwell and ends up at the hotel at long last, changes the inner layer of wet clothing for dry, and inquires about dinner,

while at the same time Hans Kristiansson is getting up from his empty coffee cup at Elina's: Now he has stalled long enough, he has to go. Like the gentleman he is, he kisses her before he leaves: she turns her face away from him, but that makes no difference. Out to the car, God, what a man he is, and the damp darkness envelops him. Off to Ramvik. Once on the highway he calms down, drives smoothly and cautiously. When he gets to Marianna, he'll tell her a thing or two. The car feels empty, the road is empty, he looks at the clock and knows he will be there in twenty minutes; he is approaching Ramvik. On Langfotvegen where Marianna lives he steps calmly out of the car, down to her door, to her window, it is dark in there, she is not at home. She is out.

And then he is struck with jealousy: "What does she think she is doing?" Nobody is waiting for him here either. Is she out making new male acquaintances? She acts like she can get along fine without him, but she has no right to just wave him away if her intention is to get someone else involved in the matter. It is his child too. Now he thinks that he would like to share the responsibility for it, and maybe the child, when it comes, will make everything simpler, maybe he'll make it (what?)——yes, everything will be simpler then. Maybe Metta knows where Marianna is. He drives toward the Bus Station Cafe, stops out front at nine thirty, what luck, at the moment he takes the keys out of the ignition he sees the legs of a girl through the glass door, a girl walking down the bright stairway. Metta Nilsen. She opens the security lock and shuts the door behind her, he rolls the window down and when she puts up her umbrella, he calls out her name,

the name of Metta Nilsen, who is coming down the stairs from the Bus Station Cafe after having finally gotten all the customers out. She has checked to see that everything is in order in the kitchen, she is on her way home to change clothes before going over for a brief visit at the restaurant of the Ramvik Hotel. Maybe she would just as soon forget the whole thing. But she has promised Marianna to come ("—as if Marianna couldn't get along without you!"). And there she was, constantly looking at the clock during her last hour of work, thinking that she could just as well not go, as tired as she was, and depressed. And she couldn't make up her mind. Restlessness ruined everything for her. The whole time she was waiting there, cursing her shift that wouldn't end, she knew that she would have almost nothing else to do at the restaurant but be a handmaiden to Marianna. Because by the time she finally got there, after a hurried change of clothes, with the smell of food from the Bus Station Cafe still in all her pores, and the sensation of marking time behind the counter still in her feet, the youth of

Ramvik would already be far into their Friday evening, the dance orchestra far into its idiotic repertoire. And the full ashtrays and the half empty bottles, the growing desperation among those who have come there to experience Something New and Great, and feel it will have to happen soon, otherwise the evening will be for naught. Metta can't stand the prospect of such an evening, but neither can she stay home. She was finally finished at the cafe, walking down the stairs: "There is nobody waiting for me, but I have to go there just the same," and the newspapers, the ones she carried under her arm, wrapped loosely in some gray paper, would have to be put in a locker in the waiting room of the Bus Station. Stay there until the next day, her day off, when she wanders from doorbell to doorbell asking if anyone wants to buy "The Class Struggle," a communist newspaper, in Ramvik. And right here: when she is about to put up her umbrella to run around the corner and put the newspapers into a metal locker, and lock them up,— here stands a huge, black Mercedes with Hans Kristiansson in it, and she ought to have said: "To hell with the whole place. I can't take anymore today!" But she walks over to the rolled down window, bends down and says "Hello, Hans, nice of you to come and pick me up." He has already opened his mouth, perhaps to ask about Marianna, but he changes his mind, and says instead: "Yes, now it's our turn." He leans across the seat and opens the door on the other side, indicates that she should go around and get in. She does, closes her umbrella, puts the newspapers on the back seat, opens her purse to hunt for a cigarette way down in the darkness: "Well, looks like you got yourself a new car today."

38

Then there is a little matter of a telephone booth in the lobby of the Ramvik Hotel, where people go to find other people. There, too, the mouthpiece gets moist after a long conversation, without the person on the other end noticing it. Also when

Henrietta Brunberg, the teacher on Eik Island, stands and talks to her husband, after having eaten a little food, after the wine has put her in a frame of mind in which she can take the whole thing more in stride, so that she can talk to him and say that he needn't worry. "We will manage. Tomorrow I'm coming home and we can discuss everything in detail,"

but when she has said hello, there is only silence at the other end, and all the bad feelings come creeping over her, like fingers around her neck, straight across the Eik Island Sound, slimy snail fingers, lurid leech fingers, and his breathing just before he bursts: "Where in the hell are you and who are you with?" She says slowly: "You are only shouting across a narrow fjord. I'm in Ramvik." "You are? Well, you can tell your new boyfriend that my advice for him is to be a little rough with you at first, then maybe you'll soften up." She says: "You have recognized your mistake, I see, Arve." And he says: "Damn right, I have." And she: "Too bad you're so miserably far off base. But I just wanted to tell you where I am." "You don't need to lie to me now, I'm finished with you, just do whatever the hell you like!" "Do you really mean that? Shouldn't we talk about things first?" "There has been more than enough talk, I don't want to see you ever again, I just don't want to see you."

But something happened there, to the telephone or Henrietta or Arve Brunberg. He stood and screamed at her right across a sound and found words he had not dared to use his whole adult life; he stood and spit into the telephone that he hated her, that is, that he could not live another day without her: "You have killed every spark of life in me, and I have never had a single day of happiness with you." She understood what he meant and let him keep talking. She only wanted to tell him that she was coming back. But he hung up before she had a chance to say anything else. Should she call him back? She decided to forget it.

Henrietta Brunberg pays for her phone call at the desk and goes over to her table in the ball room. Now it is crowded with people, talk and laughter, the ones who can dance are beginning to fill up the floor, Marianna Kretsen in her summer dress, and the fellow she is with. She sits there and looks at them, and recalls the time when she, Henrietta, was occasionally in the limelight, that spring she graduated from teachers' college and was going to go out and make herself useful in life. Because she sees a man here at the Ramvik Hotel sitting alone at a table, who resembles someone she knew back then. But *he* was much too uncultivated for her to spend her time with, and along came Arve at that point, and had his plans all set, and this place, Eik Island, way up off the northwest coast, where they would settle down and live for each other. Arve was good at talking, as long as she believed him, it was a bit like in literature, he would talk about white curtains in the summer breeze, out on the island, where the wind almost always blew in such a direction that no insects ever got near the place, where the surf came in clear colors, dark blue with huge whitecaps, the sunlight reflected off the puddles after a rain, and the hills where the sheep grazed were a thick pastel green. "Keep talking, Arve!" she said, and he talked, and she could tell that not everything he said fit together, not everything was totally genuine, but she dismissed her doubts and closed her eyes leaning back into the curve of his arm,

she sees that the man over at that table has noticed her, but why does he look down every time she looks over at him? It intrigues her that he is resisting her this way: "I may as well throw caution to the winds. After that phone call, it would not be malice toward Arve that made me seek out someone else, but my instinct for self-preservation." And at the same time she knows very well: "I'm just fantasizing. I can't get involved in anything of this sort here, who in Ramvik would dare to take home a married woman, who would dare take a man everybody knows up to her hotel room? For here, ladies and gentlemen," she thinks, "concealment is the name of the game. The point is to conceal the existence of that large chasm that opens up between men and women almost everywhere you look, to deny it, to close the window on it, so the crying will not be heard, to usher the children out so they will not have their minds corrupted by bad words. And most people will never escape from each other, they tug and pull, but the chains are there, they can't get away, and one day they can tug and pull no longer, their resistance against the living death is gone, everything is drained. They fall silent. They see each other sitting there, perhaps with sympathy because, despite everything, they once had such strong feelings for each other that they would have wished each other something more. Or: The few who go so far that one of them actually packs up his meager belongings and walks down the stairs, while the other one stands at the door and tries to cope: 'We're doing the right thing, but still, it hurts.' And they wait to cry until they are no longer in sight of each other."

39

And Marianna Kretsen, on her way back to her table after the dance, out of breath because she really threw herself into it and because they haven't had such a good orchestra in Ramvik for a long time. Fredrik, who drives the route between Ramvik and Molde, smiles at her and says that she is easy to dance with. She says: "I like being here with you." And they laugh at the expression on the face of the bass player, they noticed him when they were on the dance floor, he was no longer in this world. He moves his fingers along the neck of the instrument as he stares off into the distance, he plays well, but it is only his fingers that are working. That must be where he keeps the music ... and suddenly Marianna catches sight of a man sitting with his back partially turned toward her. He casts a glance around the room as he lights a cigarette, and she finds herself looking straight into the eyes of the Social Services Counselor she talked to earlier in the day. She thinks: "I knew it. I just suspected that nothing good would come of going out to a restaurant like *this*, it would be considered too fancy or too gauche to go out to a restaurant and pretend that nothing was wrong. Fredrik, next to her, is talking to her, telling her something or other that he has found amusing, but she does not hear what he is saying, cannot laugh along with him. He looks at her in surprise, looks away and says: "Never mind," and right afterwards he turns and asks what is wrong. But she can't confide in any more people, even though he is ever so proper and would never press her further than she herself would want. So they just sit there, something invisible has come and wedged itself between them, while everything else in the restaurant is just as before. He says: "Maybe you should have another drink." He himself is already quite high, but not so much that he could fail to note the change in her outward appearance. She shakes her head and looks at her watch: "Don't you think Metta will be arriving soon?" "I don't know," he says curtly, and wonders what that can have to do with all this. She says: "I'm sorry, Fredrik, I ... I was just thinking about something that isn't very pleasant, and that I can't tell you about. Don't worry, it will pass. Skål!" She smiles at him, makes an attempt to smile. He says briefly that she needn't be accountable to him, but that he has come here to have a good time and he intends to continue to do so. She puts her hand on his arm, "Don't be mad at me," just then Metta Nilsen appears in the doorway of the ballroom at the Ramvik Hotel,

she stands there and peers into a chaos of music and dancing bodies and lighted candles on the tables, people singing along with the music, the waiter who comes to seat her even if she is only the waitress from the Bus Station Cafe. He leads her to the table where Marianna and Fredrik are sitting and says: "I can still get you some dinner, but you'll have to make up your mind quickly." "I'll just skip it," says Metta Nilsen. And then she can turn to Marianna and give her the familiar little shove with her elbow, and Marianna looks up with a start and smiles.

Metta sees out of the corner of her eye that Fredrik is getting up from the table, he says he'll be gone a little while, he is going to dance with a girl at another table, and his whole face has a to-hell-with-girlfriends expression,

"Now don't go falling apart, Marianna, and start feeling sorry for yourself. That doesn't do any good at all."

"It was going just fine, until I caught sight of that guy over there."

Metta sees him too.

The situation is ripe for tears or a fist-fight, as exposed and vulnerable as everything is, and only alcohol protecting their thin skins. But she has to control herself, because actually the only problem is this: that she knows too much about everyone and everything here. She sees the woman who was in the cafe earlier, sitting there causing raised eyebrows by being alone so late in the evening. She sees all the others she knows only by sight. She thinks: "There is a story behind each one. If I knew everything about them I couldn't bear to sit here, and besides, no one has asked me to shoulder the whole world's grief." But she knows that now that they have all begun, cautiously, to get a bit drunk, their various troubles will all boil down to problems with their love life. And there she sits, Metta Nilsen. She sits there and has knowledge surpassing theirs, because she knows that it isn't these people there is something wrong with, but that the very conditions for love are so poor these days. They sit here with thin ice under their feet, hoping it will hold, please don't let us break through it. And she thinks that those of us who want to change this country, we need more than a theory about how money and power are interrelated. We also need insight into the inner crippling of people, into the backwards logic that controls their emotions. Here. Now. She turns toward Marianna, a pillar of stone watching the orchestra, and Fredrik whom she would like to have at her side because she is sure he only wants the best for her, but he is pulling away from her because he doesn't understand, because he isn't allowed to know. Metta says to her: "There are other people besides the Social Services Counselor here tonight who may make you feel ill at ease. Someone you know really well is out in the lobby waiting for a message from you."

She can tell that Marianna has been expecting to hear this the whole time.

"Why doesn't he just come storming in, the way he usually does?"

"I told him that he could come and sort of be my escort, if he promised to respect the fact that you are here with someone else."

"What did he say to that?"

"He said: 'I don't want to go in until Marianna comes out and says it's O.K. I don't need to make things any more difficult right now.'"

"I suppose he's drunk?"

"No, he is completely sober."

"I knew all along he would show up."

"Of course."

"Let me just think about it for a minute."

First Marianna stood up, in the ballroom at the hotel, and put her cigarettes into her purse. She smoothed the wrinkles out of her dress and looked across the dance floor to see if she could spot Fredrik. She said to Metta: "O.K. We'll be back here soon." And she walked across the floor as easily as if she were just going to the ladies' room to comb her hair.

40

A girl about 16 or 17 years old is standing in the hallway of the Brunberg's house on Eik Island, shaking the water off her clothing. It is late at night and rain is falling,

Arve Brunberg opens the door from the living room to see if it is the wind or someone else trying to play tricks on him. He sees her standing out there, his daughter Liv, kicking off her muddy footwear. He turns his head to look back at the friend of the family, who is reclining in an easy chair, snoring. He doesn't like her seeing the way things are, although she has known it for a long time. He says in a threatening voice: "Well, come on in, it's about time I had a chance to ask you if you still live here."

The girl comes into the room, notices the friend of the family and says: "Oh, so that's the way things are!" She walks out to the kitchen to find herself some food, and is busy rummaging around there when Arve comes in and announces: "And your mother, as you can see, is not at home." But the girl is not interested in knowing where her mother is, she makes some sandwiches and disappears up the stairs. He is left standing there, abandoned by his family and disdained by everyone else, that's clear to him now. Imprisoned on this island against his will, hoodwinked by a woman who once said that she loved him. He is the laughingstock of his co-workers (that, too, is clear to him now). Episode after episode flashes through his mind, each one more humiliating than the next, blunders, misunderstandings, glances people exchange behind his back: "Christ, that Brunberg!" And he sees an explanation: if he has never truly succeeded at anything, it is because he has never been able to sacrifice himself properly for his goals, because he *always* has had Henrietta's welfare in the back of his mind, disturbing every train of thought that could have led to something. He, this man who has always taken the ferry home in time to eat dinner with her, just think what he could have become... Now he sees clearly and distinctly that despite everything he has sacrificed on the family altar, the whole thing is going to the dogs, first and foremost his daughter. Isn't Henrietta even capable of seeing that? Well then, there's just no hope. He wants to test her, give her one last chance, he will call her up and ask her one last, unsentimental question: "What about our child, Henrietta? What about our child?" He makes his way over to the telephone and is about to dial the number of the hotel, his hands are shaking as he targets the little white circles on the dial one by one. There! Now she's going to get a piece of my mind, and he waits a moment to be sure that he has heard correctly: "Of course! Sure, why not? A busy signal. Maybe she's enlisted the aid of the phone company, sure, and the hotel receptionist also. Have they taken the phone off the hook so he won't be able to reach her? He needs to calm down, he knows that, just a little more and he might start laughing at himself, how ridiculous can you get . . . instead, he sinks down into a chair and contemplates what he can do, doesn't have the energy to call back again. He ought to get himself over there, pay her a surprise visit. Couldn't get there before the restaurant closes. No, that's impossible, but she would have to be at the hotel anyway, or some other place in Ramvik, there is no way for her to leave there tonight. He will appear unexpectedly, surprise her as she is rolling around in bed with someone else, not that she can't roll around with anybody she chooses, who cares, he is finished with her. But he ought to have some concrete evidence, infidelity, so she can't deny anything, then he'd have the upper hand again. He hears the blowing rain outside, it hasn't gotten any calmer in the course of the evening, and is struck by a sudden realization: "What are you contemplating! Are you going to put a boat on the water tonight? That is pure madness." And the counter argument: If there were ever a reason to risk everything, it would be now. Because his primary objective is not to surprise her. He only wants to *show* her that, no matter where she is, he can do the impossible and come and find her. The twenty-foot plastic chunk of a boat that he keeps down by the docks—he wants to go down to Olver and get help in putting it into the water, there is no one else he can ask. He knows that Olver may simply refuse, so maybe there is no risk involved? Will you be prevented from going and, at the same time, still manage to prove how much you love Henrietta? Certainly not! He has no ulterior motives! Olver will help him when he finds out what is at stake.

He puts on his coat which has been hanging over the back of a chair since he got home from work, it is damp and clammy. His umbrella is resting open in the entry hall. Sounds are coming from his daughter's record player upstairs. Should he say anything to her? Why? She has always taken her mother's side. And that slob sleeping in the chair, he ought to just kick him out. But he has more important things to attend to. The wet gusts greet him when he goes out on the steps and closes the door behind him. He may have considered taking a flashlight along, but this is no rescue mission. There is no need in this instance for high-topped boots or oilskin overcoats. He's going to a restaurant. Ha, ha. He's going to a party. He hurries on down the road, time is passing quickly. And his half-wet coat is not keeping the rain and wind out, but he is not afraid of catching his death of cold, not him, for once in his life he is living dangerously.

41

As the evening begins to move to a close the man writing asks for a bus schedule. He wants to go to Ramvik. But at the hotel desk they've never heard of the place, and the bus schedule has been touched up like everything else. So he goes to his typewriter in his room: And he strikes the keys

so that the bus driver on the Ramvik route stops dancing and walks over to Metta Nilsen and sits down.

She says to him:

"How are you? Go get your bus and drive me to Never-Never Land, and I'll buy you a beer."

And he says:

"No, but if you butter me a roll and put a slice of goat cheese on it I'll tell you why I got mad a while ago. Because after I've jostled around on these roads day in and day out and finally get a night off to go dancing I just don't have the patience for people in a bad mood. When Marianna got upset, before you came, it seemed just like it was my fault that she wasn't having a good time. I couldn't stand seeing that—that she was bored."

"And now," says Metta, "you ought to know that it has nothing to do with you and that Marianna has to be allowed to run her emotional life herself, and only then can you two be friends with each other." He beckons to the waiter to get some more drinks for Metta and himself, and breathes a sigh of relief: "We were finally beginning to get somewhere, at least that's what I would like to think. But I'm not as clever at expressing myself as you are,"

and then Metta Nilsen thinks that it's about time her day was over, and is about to ask Fredrik to dance with her. She mustn't be too condescending now, that's no good, and she mustn't isolate herself. For some reason or other she starts thinking about the guy in that poem, the one standing on Broadway and Fifth Avenue the whole day collecting money so that the poor people will have some place to sleep for the night. It's fine if they get somewhere to sleep, but that doesn't change the world, that does not change the world. She has to get involved now, before the evening is over. She has opened her mouth to speak, but changes her mind, it doesn't come automatically, not yet. She is not sitting alone with one of the bus drivers on the Ramvik route, there are others here besides them: over at a table the woman who came into the cafe earlier in the evening, at another table the Social Services Counselor, each on his own turf, sending signals to each other. But her mind is too tired to comprehend them, why doesn't she just give up. Stop playing the heroine in a children's book. Once again a reminder that she cannot solve the problems of the world alone. Next to her sits the bus driver who is supposed to be having a night off, and she thinks: "He is an O.K. guy, I have to trust him:

"Could you go over and ask that woman who is sitting alone feeling bored to dance with you, Fredrik? You can handle that, I'm sure."

"Don't you think I know who she is? Why should I bother?"

"You deserve an explanation and you'll get one later."

He says: "Alright. There's really no point in sitting here watching for Marianna." He strides across the dance floor. She sits looking at Henrietta, wondering what will happen, it seems to be going well, she lights a cigarette, and there he is, the Social Services Counselor, at her table, smiling and saying: "Good evening, would you like to dance?"

"Dance? Is that what you really want?" she asks.

He sits down.

"I don't know if you have an occupation that follows you home when the day is over."

"I sure do. You feel it in your feet after an afternoon shift at the cafe, if that's what you mean."

Some people feel it in their bodies, others in their souls.

And a bit later:

"What about you, have you got your red coat along this evening?"

"No, I only wear it when I need to make an impression on people."

"And you don't need to this evening."

"Maybe I should, but I'm too tired, I guess."

"Where did Marianna Kretsen go?"

"She's out talking to a friend."

"I wanted to tell her that the doctor I talked to after she left my office won't be persuaded this time either. But when I saw her, I just couldn't bring myself to tell her."

"Because she looked so innocent and happy?"

"Yeah, something like that."

"Tell her everything you know. Then I'll believe you respect her."

42

He stops to catch his breath in the entryway at Olver Kretsen's house, he hears someone talking softly in the kitchen, a man's voice, but he can't make out who it is. He cannot go back without carrying out his errand, he knocks on the door and steps inside, and sees the man, although the light is blinding after the walk outdoors—there sits that old codger Karl Magnus Skogmann over at the kitchen table, well into one of his ridiculous extemporaneous speeches, so far into it, in fact, that he merely nods when Arve Brunberg comes in, and completes the sentence he is in the midst of,

Olver has gotten up and is standing there, not knowing what to do with his hands. It is as if he were holding many objects and were suddenly asked to pick up a small child. He says: "Well, look who's here. You'd better sit over by the stove and see if you can get dry again. I'm just talking to Skogmann about starting on this thing tomorrow." (And he thinks: "That is fine and good, but now I don't have the energy to help Brunberg with anything at all. Tonight I can barely manage my own affairs.")

"I have to go to Ramvik immediately!" says Brunberg.

"And I have very little to offer you," Olver continues, "but you are welcome to try to coax a thimbleful out of this bottle."

"Henrietta has left me, but she hasn't gotten any further than Ramvik. I have to catch up with her there."

("Didn't I tell that man that Anna-Marja is sick, and still he comes over here and . . .")

"I talked to her this evening," says Skogmann abruptly. "It doesn't come as any surprise to me."

"No, I guess you know all about the problems of the women on this island, Skogmann. I didn't come over here to talk to you!"

"You must forgive me for chancing to sit here,"

at which point Olver Kretsen pounds three times on the table with his fist: "I don't like this discussion." He says he is glad that people drop by—"but I have responsibility for a sick wife up in the loft."

"For goodness sake, I wasn't intending on staying here," says Arve Brunberg, "I just came to ask for assistance in getting my boat into the water, but if there is no help available here, of course, I will have to manage on my own . . ."

Olver Kretsen says that he doesn't have the patience to listen to childish talk this evening. And before he can finish the sentence, he is overcome by an anger he hasn't felt for many years. He points a trembling finger at the man over by the stove: "There ought to be a limit to what a social services director can come and dish up to mature adults this late in the evening." He hears Skogmann mumbling that there is no end of occupations in this world, but he doesn't allow himself to be interrupted. Because this fellow, who sits up on the fifth floor of the Big Cross and thumbs through other peoples' misery, ought to be good enough to take care of his own. Skogmann falls silent then, and Olver heads up to the loft because he thinks he hears some moaning up there. It isn't the children, they are asleep, it is Anna-Marja. He doesn't turn on the light, but he has the feeling that she is lying with her face up against the wall: "I hear so many voices, Olver, do you have visitors down there?"

"It is just the teacher's husband, Anna-Marja, and then Skogmann, who has been here quite a while." She says: "It is shameful that I'm lying in bed like this, and I don't even know why I am doing it, I have to get up and make something to serve them. . ." He goes right up to the bed and puts a hand on her shoulder, he speaks softly, but not as if to a child: "I have told them that you aren't feeling well today, and neither one of them wanted anything to eat. You just lie quietly now, they'll be leaving soon, and I'll come up again."

"I hope you didn't say it was nerves, did you?"

"No, I didn't say it was nerves," he lies and finds it totally justified to lie. "Can you do me a favor and rest here quietly?" She complains far down in the pillows that, "I always do what you tell me." "This time, too," he says, "I'll be back soon." He closes the door. Brunberg looks up and is set for a rebuttal: "You needn't be on your high horse, Kretsen, I happen to know that your daughter is getting drunk and offering herself to everything in pants at the Ramvik Hotel, so you have a problem or two to take care of yourself!"

Skogmann makes a move to stand up and says: "Look, I think that . . ."

"Sit down, Karl Magnus," says Olver Kretsen tersely. He turns to the other man: "Marianna can go out to the hotel as often as she wants as far as I am concerned (while inside he feels irritated: 'So that's where she is this evening'), but thanks for letting me know where I can get hold of her, there have been a lot of telephone messages for her this evening. . ." He goes to the telephone to call the hotel, while Skogmann sits looking at Brunberg until he says: "I wanted to tell you that I talked with Henrietta last night,"

and when Olver Kretsen comes back from making the phone call, Skogmann is busy giving a piece of his mind to Arve Brunberg. He tells him that it must be about a hundred years since anyone drowned in the sound between Eik Island and Ramvik, there was a boat crew of six men who were going over after some barrels of flour for Christmas and suddenly a wind came up and four of the men were never found, but two of them had gotten their arms stuck in the oar locks so that they were found floating with the boat. "But they went over to get flour for the people here, and there had been bad weather for days. They went because it was a necessity, and nobody could say afterwards that they had been daredevils." And then there was a story about a priest who had used Moses and the Red Sea as a text at their funeral, and about how he had a vision of a bridge or a road from Eik Island to Ramvik, so that people could walk across without getting their feet wet. But people walking home from the cemetery said: "We better stick to the old-fashioned way of getting flour, however good his idea about a bridge may be,"

for they had moved out there because the fish were thick in the sea that swirled aimlessly in the nearby skerries, because the patches of grass among the rock outcroppings on the island were green. And for the sake of the mild winters.

"Do you think this winter will be a mild winter?"

Then Arve Brunberg says:

"Excuse me for intruding. I just lost control for a while. I'll go back home now." Olver Kretsen says: "It's gotten colder, I see."

The rain changes into sleet.

The white flakes are sticking to the window panes.

He thinks about some root crops he still has in the ground out in the garden. He has set out to make a living, to make a go of it here in this place. He thinks about how it will be if Anna-Marja has to be sent away. But at least the roof is on, protection against another drafty winter. The small things are all set. Then there is everything else.

"We'll have to get together later tomorrow," he says, "to talk about what we are going to do to stop *them*." Skogmann says: "Count me in." Arve Brunberg: "I don't know if I can muster the energy to get involved in anything at all." Skogmann again: "It is a crucial job and we need help. From you, too." Brunberg: "I don't even know how long I'll be staying on this island." Skogmann again: "Better hope they have jobs in the place you're considering moving to. Even though you yourself haven't been involved with them . . ." And Brunberg: "Thank you very much. May I ask you to call me?"

They both leave, the ground is already white. Outside, they part to go their separate ways. Olver can just make them out through the kitchen window. He turns around when they have gone, removes the empty bottle, and looks to see if there are other things he ought to clean up, those dirty dishes he put on the kitchen counter, before he climbs up the stairs to the woman he lives with,

Skogmann on the way down toward the wharves, past the tree, home to the dark house, where he lights the lamp above the table and sits down to read in a book he has borrowed. A book about his own era and its social-democratic perspectives. He sits, staring out into the fjord, as if his eyes could manage to discover something on the other side. But he sees nothing, except the white sleet on the window pane. And the showers of white on every new page he turns to,

Brunberg on the way home to the teacher's house, as everyone on the island calls it: "It is not his house, he just lives there." He thinks: "Our friend of the family must be gone by now, and if not, I'll ask him to leave,"

Olver Kretsen has gone up to Anna-Marja, the wind is playing rough with the wooden beams above his head, he stands there undressing in the dark and hoping she is asleep, because he doesn't know if he has anything to say to her. He pulls his undershirt up over his head and feels the sweaty spots from beneath the armpits glide along his upper arms toward his elbows. Anna-Marja says: "Are they still down there, I seem to hear them talking on and on." "No, they have gone." Then the telephone rings, she sits bolt upright and he says: "It is only Marianna, I asked her to call." He goes down to speak to her very calmly and not frighten her,

Brunberg puts the key in the lock and sees that the friend of the family has not left, his coat is still in the entryway. He goes into the living room, he is not there. Brunberg starts up the stairs to the loft. Up in his daughter's room the record player is mumbling on and on.

Down by the wharves Karl Magnus Skogmann is staring out into the driving sleet,

Olver Kretsen carefully replaces the receiver and hears Anna-Marja asking him from upstairs: "Is there something wrong with Marianna?"

But through the door the music reaches Arve Brunberg in the narrow passageway along the loft, he moves nearer to listen, he hears the low, embarrassed laughter and protests of his daughter, the friend of the family whispering and breathing audibly, and Arve Brunberg walks into his empty bedroom and throws himself down on the bed. He screams, but no sound comes out of his mouth.

43

The evening is approaching an end at the Ramvik Hotel, and the man writing has gone out into the rain. He follows the street until he sees the light from the salons at the Alexandra Hotel, but wishes he were in Ramvik. He sweeps his right hand through the air, and the ballroom appears, with Metta Nilsen and all the others. They are among the people in the ballroom there, and everything is becoming looser and looser beneath the fake antique chandeliers in the ceiling, a whirring wheel beneath them, a carousel, the music and people singing along, a disc revolving up on the stage by the orchestra with a red light behind it, and red beams passing over the dancers. There sits the Social Services Counselor for Ramvik, Halvor Børresen, talking with Metta Nilsen. She has been expecting him to dance with her, but he does not ask her a second time. And she silently curses all the men who think that a smart woman has no desire to dance. He asks: "Could I maybe invite some of you home with me this evening?" She answers: "Go ahead, but right now I would like to dance." However, exactly at that moment the music stops and Fredrik comes walking over with Henrietta, they look toward the table with some uncertainty, and have apparently been discussing matters. "Park yourselves here!" calls Metta, and they come over. The Social Services Counselor, the perfect gentleman, gets up to shake hands with Henrietta. "You look so familiar to me, and I was wondering if you weren't..." "Arve Brunberg's wife," says Henrietta, and he says: "Right," and she: "Maybe I am, and maybe I'm not,"

"join our party," urges Metta, "and now I *demand* to dance!" She drags Fredrik out onto the dance floor and knows that the two they have left behind will be searching awkwardly for a conversation topic, but everything in the world will get squared away sooner or later. Fredrik says: "You seem different. Have you been drinking too much?" "No, too little, much too little!" And he laughs back: "You going to stick it out for the whole party after all?" "You better believe it!" she says, and starts singing the Swedish winner in the Grand Prix Melody Contest "Damn, If This Doesn't Look Like Love!"

and she notices, as she lays her head on his shoulder for a moment of oblivion, that Marianna Kretsen is walking onto the dance floor with

Hans, and Metta cannot forget what she said to him in the car, the only thing she will never be able to tell Marianna,

they were driving around in the short streets of Ramvik, she was trying to explain to him in brief, because occasionally in life one begins to run out of words. She had said:

"I am not asking you to be noble. I am asking you to think about yourself. Because what you do tonight, I don't think you will ever be able to do over again,"

and then she sat in the car and waited for him while he went to his room and changed clothes. He came down again and mumbled: "I know you are right, of course." And he drove to the hotel, went into the lobby with her, said: "I'll sit and wait out here."

Marianna, dancing there, and Hans a short distance away from her, not looking at her, but not looking away either. She stares at his hands, the way she did that time he was repairing the record player, the day she sat on the roof of the cafe kitchen and watched him climbing on the building next door. It is a time for reminiscence, time to take leave of something that is *past*, she sees him climbing the wall, she sees the houses along the street in the center of Ramvik, post-war houses, grown up out of the bare dirt. And it strikes her that all along, the whole time she has been here in Ramvik and Eik Island, things have been happening to her, *to* her. This is really the first time she has had a chance to ask herself what she actually wants. Now things are as they should be, she smiles to him, just as they should be. Maybe he smiles back, at any rate he is looking at her now

this guy who knows that he is going to leave her alone and not bother her any more unless *she* wants him to. He thinks about the day that will soon be over. The drive through the rain. He thinks about Elina and sees her head buried in the white pillow, what has he done to her, was he really the one who did it? the one who visited his father's office, was that him? He feels divided in half, with one of his feet stuck in the morals he inherited from his social class, where they do nothing but steal: turn someone on with one hand and steal with the other—money, love. All this, which he has carried further in the same way to its only logical consequence: desperation, delinquency. On another narrow ledge of rock rests his other foot. So there he stands, teetering, trying from time to time to discover if he has anything else inside him that might serve as a better foundation. He has looked around for someone to talk to, someone who will say: "Hey, never mind, man, we understand." He is balancing there now, but can it last? He needs to get away somewhere for a while. While there is still time.

A teacher by the name of Henrietta Brunberg at a table at the Ramvik Hotel, who has spent the evening realizing that she is almost forty. She has seen the young girls on the dance floor, and felt that maybe it was their music being played here. She has vacillated between desperation and amazement, between the thought she doesn't dare pursue: "What have I missed?" and the strings she is clutching in the hand gripping her glass, between the things she knows about herself and the life she has been sentenced to live. "In a couple of years, if we don't move, maybe our daughter Liv will be sitting here in this same spot. Will her body be tugged in two directions like this? I have to help prevent it."
But even greater is her responsibility to herself, because she cannot take the easy route back, back to *once upon a time,* before his smile for her hardened into an evil grimace and he clenched his teeth. This fellow sitting next to her now, talking about the town and the people, he is younger, he is a handsome man, he is so well-mannered, without being reserved, although he never comes right out with the point he is making, but appears instead as though the world had recently come crashing down on his head and he were sitting there calmly trying to ascertain what hit him.
"Maybe we should dance after all?" she asks, and they leave the table. Join the young people. Her partner's elegant manner irritates her, but she knows that she doesn't yet dare to be anything but elegant herself. What would happen if she really let her hair down . . . The evening is drawing to a close. The man at the organ is thanking them for a lovely evening. And that's that. The lights come on brightly everywhere in the ballroom, they go to their tables and pay their bills. They wonder where they can get a taxi in this rain, but Hans has a big enough car for everyone. Only Metta Nilsen is left wandering around howling, in Swedish, that "damn, if it doesn't look like love." They just

think she has drunk too much and pay no attention to her. She would never do anything wrong anyway, now would she?

Out in the cloak room they are paging Marianna Kretsen, there is a message for her, she is to call home. Marianna walks palefaced to the phone booth. Finally she catches up with the others waiting in the car, headlights on, she gets in, squeezes into the back seat without a word. Henrietta, who suddenly sees the truth, tries to say as quietly as possible: "It is the wretched souls of Ramvik riding home with you tonight, Mr. Social Services Counselor." No one answers, Henrietta feels a prickle of embarrassment because she has said something dumb, while Metta Nilsen recites in a monotone, as if she had just learned to spell: "Damn, if it doesn't look like love."

44

And the rain, says the man writing, that rain I have been writing about for so long, has turned to sleet, to large white flakes that melt instantly in people's hair, turn to water on their overcoats and have to be brushed off with the palms of their hands. At the same time that he is approaching Ramvik in a taxi

people are getting out of a car by the apartment complex on the outskirts of Ramvik, and walking toward the gate with the Social Services Counselor Halvor Børresen in the lead. Keys out of his jacket pocket, in through the outer door. There they stand in the new, white hallway, their eyes are getting accustomed to the light after the drive over, their footsteps echo as they climb the stairs. They try not to make any noise—and up there in the entryway: the women bend down and pull off their high-top boots, coats, umbrellas stretched taut and dripping on the bathroom floor, small rivers of autumn in Ramvik on their way toward the drain and on out to sea. In the warmth of the living room, lights being turned on, a shelf filled with music on large-diameter records. Metta heads there immediately: "You don't have that record they were playing at the hotel, do you, the Swedish one?" She starts

THE FERRY CROSSING

thumbing through them. The man who lives in this apartment asks Marianna to help him carry some glasses in from the kitchen. They go out there—this is taking place on one of the upper floors—and look out over Ramvik, toward the Big Cross, a black colossus, and beyond it: the big floodlights on the ferry landing. He stands for a long time absentmindedly holding three or four long-stemmed glasses between his fingers, looking out, Marianna doesn't know what she should do, so she blurts out that: "You are surely agile enough to manage the serving without me!" To which he places the glasses carefully on the counter and tells her straight out that he thinks her chances of getting an abortion are essentially zero. She sort of nods her head because she is just as aware of that as he is, and he asks what she intends to do, if she is going to try to do it illegally. She cannot, or will not, answer him. He asks if Hans is the one, she nods, and then he says: "If your final decision is that you cannot take on a child, I will try to help you all the same. Maybe there is some solution." "We better go in with the others, I guess," she says, and takes some of the things he has set out. They come in, Metta has put on a record, but very low so that they can talk above it. Fredrik glances around after more refreshments, he must not be used to impromptu parties of this sort, and Metta sits down next to Hans to put some semblance of order into the whole mess. What can Hans do in this situation, he

is forced to tell them an anecdote, he is feeling that the premises on which he has built the evening are getting rather shaky, since the thing he really wants to do is take Marianna into a room where they can have a decent conversation. He may as well tell them about the drive he made from Molde to Bud and back to the cafe on the mountainside,

where he meets this man who is writing in a book, a man he drops off at the house where his parents live. God only knows if he has found his way back to Oslo,

and at that point the doorbell rings. They look at each other and at their host, who says with the voice of a telephone operator "Mission Hotel, Night Clerk, may I help you?" and then tells them to stop laughing. "Shall I let in more wretched souls?" "If it is my husband, don't let him in," says Henrietta. They ask if he is on this side of the sound. "No, but I feel like he is following me all the time."

That's how Henrietta Brunberg got the party going while Halvor Børresen was downstairs seeing who was at the door. Marianna turned to Hans and said: "I have almost no chance of getting an abortion, he says." "I had no idea. I'm sorry," said Fredrik and clutched his glass. Marianna turned to Fredrik and said: "I have never been so glad for anything as when you asked me out this evening." The door to the hallway was standing open. They heard Halvor Børresen coming up the stairs, talking to a man. Henrietta said to Marianna: "Nothing surprises me around here,"

and there he stood, in the doorway. And Hans was the one who slapped his forehead with a little laugh and made room on the couch where he was sitting: "Come in, man, come on in. I was just telling them about you."

And the man writing sees a motley collection of people in a room, and there is always a secret hope in such situations. That he may write their stories, that they are worth being written. He says: "I am looking for someone who writes romantic novels for women, he wouldn't happen to be..." "Yes, that's him, that's him!" screams one of the people sitting there, the others are dying laughing, and she crows a line from a Swedish song: "Damn, if this doesn't look like love!"

45

And he tells about the intolerable thought of a yellow sign, posted on one of the roads leaving Molde, with the name *Ramvik* written on it in black letters, and a number showing how many kilometers he still has to go. And maybe what was once a falsification of the map in the stairwell of the Romsdalsheimen Hotel is now correct. But all the busses to Ramvik had gone when he finally realized what he had to do. He walked to the taxi stand by the Romsdalsheimen, where the drivers had lined up, waiting for people on whom the evening had taken its toll. And they argued about who ought to get this next passenger, because it is quite profitable to get a long distance traveller when business is slow. At last he was seated in a taxi that turned out onto the bumpy road, into the murky night, with a driver who switched on the radio so they could catch the last news broadcast before they got to Ramvik. They talked about a big operation to be started out on the islands, and he said to himself: "If you just wait a bit, you'll get your story gratis." The driver asked him where he should drop him. At a hotel or a guest house, if he didn't know where Hans Kristiansson lived.

The driver drove to the Ramvik Hotel. There was little activity there, apart from the waiters cleaning up after people had gone home, and an old night clerk sitting in the lobby, thumbing through a newspaper (which was incorrect). He looked down at the guest register and said: "Yes, there we have it, Arve Brunberg!" He could just as well answer yes, it really makes no difference what your name is, but he absolutely had to get hold of Hans Kristiansson. Had he been there that evening?

What a coincidence: "He just drove off in a car with your wife, not long before you came through the door." He put his suitcase down and asked if anyone knew where they were going, because he felt he was on the right track.

The night clerk asked him to wait. He would ask the waiter. The man writing sat in a chair in the lobby and felt himself growing impatient. He had been on their trail for a long time now. At that point the night clerk returned: "They went home with the Social Services Counselor. Should I take your suitcase up first?" He said thank you and gave him the bag, and got a taxi: "Drive me to the apartment of the Social Services Counselor for Ramvik."

The driver pressed a button and asked on the mobile telephone: "Where does Halvor Børresen live now?" He got the address. But the dispatchers did not know if he was at home, since he had left the hotel in a car with Hans Kristiansson and some other people. "Pretty soon now you'd better start taking notes," thought the man writing.

And there he is, standing in the doorway, looking in at them.

46

There is a woman sitting on a sofa in an apartment in a complex on the outskirts of Ramvik. She says: "Well, you roving bandit, you aren't at the end of the trail yet. Beyond this farce of a small town lies an island, with more than fifty people on it. A ferry runs out there, taking people back and forth on a fixed schedule, which you have to observe. The ferry doesn't wait.

But if you get off at the old landing over there, and follow the road all the way to the top, you will see a rather new house, built about fifteen years ago, so that a young couple can go over there on the ferry with a load of suitcases, and a little child, everything you need to fill a house with. They can go ashore there, stand and look around, be received by the storekeeper, who is a member of the school board and is going to show them around, shake hands and offer them a large hand cart to put their baggage on. Up the hill to the new house which stands there gleaming brightly with new wood and smelling clean inside, suitcases on the floor there, in the entryway, and a tour of each room: this is where we will live. This is where we will carry out our mission. And the first months, full of conversations about everything new, everything that must be done, and a child who demands all the time outside of the school day. A man who gets a job on this side of the fjord and is involved in the administration of the municipality, and a woman who is asked over and over again to provide leadership for the small community on all solemn occasions and in all common concerns, she can't manage to live up to that. She gives up after a rather short period, because she doesn't share their views on life, life as an open book she should fill to overflowing with socially constructive deeds, she can't do it. She thus limits her activities to the duties she is paid for, and as their child gets older and the daily routine less strenuous, she has time to look up, look around. She sees nothing more than a couple dozen houses, with people doing what they have to do, and a husband who stumbles through the door around four-thirty each afternoon. She has been waiting for him since she came from school, has had time to think about what they can do in their free time. She has been thinking: Today I will talk to him about what happened at school, tell him how I feel, ask his advice if there is the slightest thing I need to ask about, then we'll have something to share. Something that will grow and perhaps spawn a new conversation tomorrow, and I will ask him about his life during the hours we are apart. Most importantly it must be understood that he is tired, that he may be irritated, that there are many difficult cases he has to take a stance on in the course of his day, that it has nothing to do with me if he is unapproachable and on edge when he comes home. I will take it in stride, be patient. Then he comes, he reads the newspaper at the dinner table, I ask if he would like coffee and he says yes. Then he asks me if there is more cake, but by then I, too, am into the newspaper. I explain to him where he can find it, and he gets up disgruntled: 'Is that how it is around here . . .' I ask if it is unreasonable that he be asked to get a few things for himself, since we both work, and he answers: 'I didn't say a word, dear! Not a word!' 'You did, too,' I say, and he says: 'Are we going to start arguing now?' 'This is not an argument!' I scream, 'I'm just trying to talk to you!' 'Talk, my foot!' he says, and goes up to take a nap, knowing he'll be gone an hour and a half. But the whole time I sit listening for him to come back down and dreading it. That's how it was before. Now?

I have started doing as I please. I have been away from him several nights, but I never do anything that would hurt him, except to allow him to believe that I'm involved with other people. Tonight I was at the Ramvik Hotel and then I rode over here, and as we drove up just now I sat squeezed in between these two girls in the back seat and I saw people on the way home from their Friday evening, and amidst the lonely men with umbrellas and gray suits, every time we drove past one of them I had a sinking feeling: "That's him. That's him!" Of course, it wasn't him. But I see him everywhere. In two short days my twelve pupils at the Eik Island Elementary School will rise courteously at their desks the moment I enter the classroom, and here I sit and don't know what is going to happen,"

and the woman talking turns to a younger girl who is also sitting there, and says: "What are you thinking of doing, Marianna," and the other girl answers: "I told you, didn't I, I just don't know,"

but he sees that everyone around the table is thinking the same thing, that someplace or other there must be a man, a doctor or a quack, who will open a back door when all the others are closed, to a room where there is no other equipment than the bare essentials for the removal of a fetus, a man who takes the money first, and clumsily or professionally accomplishes what a small-town, Norwegian cafe waitress is forced to ask for,

...and there is also another situation worth giving some thought to: the two or three men who will soon sit down around a table and decide if there are grounds for removal of a fetus from the body of a girl from Eik Island, they will consider how it would be to live alone and try to get to your evening shift in a cafe when there is a baby crying in a crib in your one-room flat. For them this is merely business, their job to make such decisions. And they go home to supper when the final word has been uttered at their meeting, sworn to silence as always. In the dark of night, after they have switched off the lamps above the bed, perhaps they talk to their wives about the many difficult decisions now weighing on their shoulders. But on the other hand: doesn't it usually prove true that when a mother is forced, so to speak, to complete a pregnancy, doesn't she normally take care of the child when it comes, doesn't she take the screaming bundle in her arms and think: "What could I have been thinking when I wanted to have *you* aborted?" These men think life is sacred, always, unless, of course, the hand of misfortune is at work and mows down a child on a dark road some evening—that is something different, even if the mother happens to be at her evening shift at the Bus Station Cafe just then,

...And he hears the person named Fredrik say: "Strange times we live in, strange times," while Hans Kristiansson sits looking at Marianna unable to say anything at all. He would perhaps have liked to say: "You don't need to be alone with the baby," and she could have answered: "How do you expect me to rely on you? I can't take it upon myself to raise you, too." And then Henrietta could have said that the decision ought to be Marianna's alone: "And anybody who feels the need to get involved, better also be willing to help Marianna find a doctor." And she would continue that it is odd that Marianna is old enough to wear herself out in the Bus Station Cafe for practically no pay, but not old enough to be in charge of her own body and, worse still, will never be old enough. But they don't talk about Marianna any more,

Henrietta Brunberg has been drinking industriously since she arrived, and now she mumbles: "There's just no end to all this, I can feel myself sitting here listening for Arve to show up. And now, Metta Nilsen, I can see you are really restless, too. What's that all about?" "Metta is a communist," says Marianna, and is beginning to get a bit drunk herself. "Can I call my mother at this time of night? She is lying in the loft, moaning, my father told me on the phone." But Metta says: "What's so crazy about me being a communist? Marianna!" ("Come on, Metta, I didn't mean anything by that.") And Fredrik says: "Hell, you're still a human being."

But Metta Nilsen over there, he can tell there is something eating at her. And she could have told them that it's just that she has to get up early the next day, she could have told them about the newspapers in the locker at the Bus Station Cafe, waiting to be distributed, from a spot she has chosen in front of the Bus Station Cafe. Or from door to door in the apartment houses in Ramvik. She gets up without speaking and the other says: "Hey, what's your hurry, you know you can't leave us now!" But she has to go and Hans offers to drive her. "You are drunk," she says, he shakes his head: "I'll drive you." To the others he says that he will be right back, and then he and Metta disappear.

The man writing notes that Halvor Børresen is no longer being secretive about his intentions with Henrietta and she makes no attempt to hide her response to his questions, although she is frightened. They dance, and Fredrik is left trying to put some life back into Marianna, maybe he should try to carry on a conversation with the author, who is sitting there lethargically observing

that Hans has returned after driving Metta home and sat down and started drinking with a vengeance, with Fredrik, but without speaking, while Marianna is falling asleep in the chair. Henrietta and the Social Services Counselor are dancing their way into the bedroom, and he sticks his head out again: "Just drink as much as you like, it comes out of the social services budget!" They shrug their shoulders and smile when he is gone: "Was he *that* horny?" "Didn't you see his eyes the whole night?" And Hans and Fredrik most likely keep on drinking, the man writing gets up and says uncertainly: "I'd best be getting back to the hotel," when Henrietta suddenly calls from the bedroom: "Take my room, then it will get some use," and he shuffles out into the entryway to find his coat and hears Fredrik say behind him: "Shouldn't we wake up Marianna? And what was it you were telling me about Metta?"

"It was so strange," says Hans, "she asked me to go up to her room with her. I said no, it was simply the case that I was dead tired after all this. But I had never expected such an invitation from her,"

and the man writing hobbles down the stairs and out into the clear air. He pauses outside the building and sets a course to the Ramvik Hotel.

47

He opens the curtain on the third and final day of his story. He wakes up in a hotel room in his new municipality, Ramvik, gets up and goes to the window to look out. Before he has taken the book he is writing out of his bag he sees nothing, but with the white pages in front of him he sees this: the streets, the sidewalk, and the little gardens outside are covered with a thin layer of wet snow, where the cars make parallel, black tracks and children in their rubber overalls try to scrape together enough for snowballs and snow statues. He sees

a swing still in motion after the child who has been sitting on it has jumped out. He sees the water out there, black waves rolling up to the wharves, and the ferry coming from the island he has put in place,

then he can close the book again, *the ferry*, he has written, is coming over from Eik Island with "its white wreath around the bow." Skogmann is on board, placing his hat on the table in the salon and looking around

at the housewives who are going to Ramvik to shop, now that it is Saturday and they have their husbands at home and can get away, they buy coffee at the window because that's part of their outing, and sit there talking about ordinary things while the slush on their boots melts, forming puddles on the deck. Skogmann should have talked to all of them, he could have been entertaining the women with all the strange things he says, or directed their thoughts toward something important. Today he is not capable of it. He takes something to read out of his bag, a book he has borrowed: social democratic perspectives on the country and the island where he lives, fails to find anything relevant, he shuffles up on deck, stands looking back, it's true, the island looks different with the white film of wet snow, but has no connection with the material he is reading. And he gives a sudden start and stares, the boat that disappeared when the bad weather came has returned, and lies docked, gray and ugly, at the end of the island. Will there soon be more blasting? He wants to put a stop to that, he has to talk some sense into them. When the ferry has arrived in Ramvik he goes ashore and shuffles around for a while among the houses there, waiting until an appropriate time for his errands. He looks into the stores, the merchants are having sales on summer clothing at this time of year, the windows are full of signs, everything has its price, swimwear in pastels, summer shirts with short sleeves, and in the next window: sandals, summer shoes, air mattresses, plastic beach balls to blow up, to fill with the empty air surrounding him and toss out into the sea to drift around,

outside a tobacco shop fresh local papers hang on the racks, frozen, he goes in and buys them, and afterwards shuffles up the stairs to the Bus Station Cafe, sits down in a corner to peruse them, the notices about the big industrial project on Eik Island, the picture of the mayor of Ramvik and the interview with the assistant director of the concern that is going to establish itself on his coast: that nothing has been definitely decided yet, everything depends on so many factors, but the municipality of Ramvik is showing great interest and would offer a readily accessible labor market,

Skogmann looks at the clock: Now I must make the most of my time. He puts on his coat, walks across the square to the main entrance of the Big Cross. But the door is locked. Through the glass panes he can make out a person inside, it's the watchman, who opens the door a crack and asks what the old man wants:

"I have to speak with Mayor Jacobsen. There is an important matter I must discuss with him . . ."

One has to understand that he is not there today, everyone takes Saturdays off in that building.

"This is very important."

"You could try to call him at home if it is that important. But if I were you, I wouldn't bother the mayor on his day off."

Then he walks back across the square, up to the Bus Station Cafe, had been hoping that Marianna Kretsen would be there, she could have helped him get where he wanted to go, she knows her way around Ramvik so well. But Marianna is not there. Instead he asks to use the telephone in the kitchen and calls, is told that the mayor is at a meeting, and is not expected back until late in the afternoon,

he sits down to think about what he should do now: "I guess I just won't get to talk to him today . . ." He thinks about whom he could call to a gathering, besides Olver and the teacher's husband. Are there maybe a few others he can count on over on Eik Island? He jots some names on his napkin with his fountain pen, the ink runs so the names are almost illegible, but he writes a couple more, and drinks pensively from his coffee cup, until he

happens to look out the window and a taxi is stopping on the square outside. Out comes the mayor with two other men. They unlock a side door to the Big Cross and go in, it appears as if the mayor says something amusing as he lets them in. Skogmann has stood halfway up to open the window and shout at them to wait for him, or at least knock on the window in hopes that he will be heard, but it is too late, he slumps slowly down into his chair: "I guess I won't get to talk to them this time after all."

48

"With a white wreath of foam around its bow." The man writing turns around toward the room he is in, which seems rather dark after looking at all the whiteness outside. There is an open suitcase on the bench by the door. A woman has left some articles of clothing hanging over the end of the bed, a pair of panty hose and a wrinkled brown dress,

he asks himself if the conclusions people draw so automatically are worth anything at all. In any case he has to get done in the course of the day. When he has ordered coffee from room service he realizes it will soon be ten o'clock and that the people up at the Social Services

Counselor's apartment need to be awakened soon. Henrietta Brunberg will soon be finding herself in a strange bed in a dimly lit room, she will lie there for a while before it dawns on her where she is, and a diffuse

sense of remorse will grip her, she won't be able to put her finger on just why, a remorse as strong as if she had left a child outside and gone indoors for the night or something. She looks to her side. The man lying there is in the process of waking up, she looks down at her body before she jumps out of bed and starts getting dressed, quickly and silently, as

she pulls the long party dress over her head he opens one eye over there in the bed and looks at her with a blank expression, gets up with a start, turns to her and says:

"Hello, may I introduce myself, the Social Services Counselor for the municipality of Ramvik." He extends his hand and she has to laugh,

"How many wretched souls do you have in your care this morning?" He doesn't know. He hops into his pants and asks: "You weren't thinking of leaving just like that, were you? That's not allowed, you know." She says: "I don't know, and I don't even know where I'm going." He: "We'll have breakfast here," and he walks out into the living room where

Marianna Kretsen is lying on the sofa asleep with her childlike face sticking out from beneath a blanket, and next to it that loyal watch dog Hans Kristiansson, asleep in the chair. Fredrik is gone. Halvor Børresen rolls up the shade and shouts: "Now it's morning. Up and at 'em!" Marianna moans and turns over. Hans gets up and hurtles toward the bathroom to splash some water on his face, put his exterior in order, a necessary formality now that he has adopted a new image,

then he notices the car parked casually on the lot outside, which was supposed to be delivered in Molde at nine o'clock and about which, at this very moment, he couldn't give a damn. He tells Marianna that he has to go, she looks at him and asks if it is necessary, "just when we might be able to talk," but he *must* go, thinks about trying to borrow some money from someone here, but that too is now an impossibility, so he apologizes for having to rush off, goes down the steps, has trouble getting the motor to start,

finally gets the car out of the frozen crust and onto the road, when it hits him,

Metta Nilsen, she's the only one he knows that he can possibly ask a favor of from now on, he goes to the house where she lives and hops up the freshly scrubbed stairs to her room, leaving a trail of wet footprints behind him,

"I should have been up a long time ago," she thinks bitterly as she stands there in front of the large mirror in the hall, drying herself after her shower. The doorbell rings,

and she opens the door a crack, lets him in without a moment's concern, he stops short for a moment on the floor of the entryway and gapes at her: "Have you gotten into self-discovery now too!" He hears "Yo-o-ou, too!" in Swedish and walks into her room to wait, "what does he want this time," she thinks, wondering if she should apologize for having invited him up last night, but that's out of the question!

"Yo-o-ou, too!" says the record player, and she goes over and lifts the needle after she has gotten her clothes on, "what do you want?" He says he needs to borrow some money, "how much?" a "hundred crowns," that's nearly all she has, but she opens a rickety, blue drawer and gives him the crisp new bill, he looks uncertainly at her before he sticks it in his inside pocket and says: "You will get it back," "of course, I will get it back," she says, "where do you intend to go now?" He explains, she asks when he'll be back, and then stands still and listens as he hurtles down the stairs and disappears.

Then she starts her pilgrimage through Ramvik's streets to roust out the two sleeping high-school students and a warehouse employee who has already arrived at the breakfast table: everybody be at my place at eleven, not a second later. On the way to the luggage locker at the Bus Station, where her newspapers are stored, she wonders if the gathering at the home of the Social Services Counselor has broken up, but doesn't have time to stop by Marianna's place.

Her whole body is tired and listless. It makes her ponder about why she approaches her tasks with such aversion: Maybe, when you get right down to it, she has not understood much of this thing they call communism, it ought to be a pleasure to carry out her work, every step she takes ought to be like one step closer to the society of the future.

Or is it the way she approaches the work, wearing herself out, although she doesn't get much accomplished, trying to pull herself and others around by the hair, nagging and pestering. She goes up the stairs to her flat, makes coffee and gulps down a quick breakfast, starts preparing for the meeting while she waits for the others to arrive. The pile of newspapers to be divided up is lying on the table in front of her.

It strikes her that she has often gone out to sell the newspaper without having had time to read it in advance herself, she has gone around spreading a political viewpoint she herself hasn't had time to become familiar with, and she chances to think about once this winter when

she was standing, looking at the clock impatiently, thinking that the guy who was supposed to sell newspapers with her most likely wasn't going to show up. He was to have rung every other doorbell in the apartment buildings, but he didn't come, she would have to manage the large complex alone, she has to go all alone, she thinks that is pitiful. She ends up in a heated debate behind the front door of a man who is only too happy to talk to her because he is sitting home alone this particular evening with a sleeping child, this bald-headed man in his forties, who would never in his wildest dreams have thought of talking politics in his leisure time. But here he stands, willing to do whatever it takes to get a person to stay and talk to him. He says:

"Come and sit down and convince me. Then maybe I'll buy a newspaper from you."

"I have to ask the other people in this unit, too, before I call it quits, and I can't ring their doorbells much later than this." She looks at her watch, at the pile of newspapers resting on her arm, at the man talking and at the walls around them,

"If you don't allow yourselves any time to talk to people, you'll never get anywhere with your proselytizing!"

"But I have to go out of town tomorrow and be gone for nearly three weeks . . . I have to distribute these newspapers tonight!"

"You could surely continue when you get back, couldn't you?"

"But by then a new paper would be out!"

"What?"

"The newspaper would have put out a new edition by then."

"Oh, I see."

"It's not that I don't want to talk to you, I would like to very much!"

"It seems as if you are in a hurry to save people's souls!"

"No . . ."

"In a hurry, I said!"

"No!"

And she says a bit more softly: "Can't I just try the other people around here first? I would prefer to come back to you when I'm finished. It won't take such a long time . . ."

"You won't come back!"

"I promise that I'll come! The sooner you let me go, the sooner I'll be back." She leaves, she can feel his eyes following her mistrustfully up the stairs to the next floor. She goes to another unit and sells one more newspaper, but it will soon be too late, after ten o'clock there is no use ringing the doorbells in Ramvik. She makes her way back to the fellow who is sitting there, waiting for her. She is afraid of ringing the wrong bell, stopping at the wrong floor, but it's him alright, smiling over his triumph. They sit down to talk, he wants to offer her a drink, but she refuses. He is drinking while he creates his arguments. She could have saved herself the trouble, the distance between them is too great to be closed in an evening, he must be a businessman, he knows far too many statistics, which he keeps tossing in her face: "Did you know that? No, I didn't think you would! How people can get involved in politics when they know so little..." She answers that maybe it isn't just a matter of knowing statistics, but she isn't getting anywhere, "and won't even take a drink, puritanical to boot." Luckily his wife comes sailing in at that moment, looks angrily at Metta and wants to know what is going on, and her husband says: "We were just having a discussion about something." He follows her to the door, at any rate, and gives her the money for the newspaper,

there is a cautious rap at the door, she looks at her watch and sees that it is five to eleven, the warehouse worker floats silently through the door, and behind him footsteps can be heard on the stairs, one of the high school students. They look around because her place is a mess, and sit down to read the new issue of *The Class Struggle*. She doesn't wait a single second for the last person. After a couple of small announcements she tells the story of Marianna and Hans, just the essentials, and the eyes of one of them grow wide because he is so young that he has never been close to a problem like this before, and the warehouse man sucks on his pipe: "That's a hell of a mess."

"I'm not asking your opinion of the matter," says Metta curtly, "I am asking what I ought to do, and if what I have done so far is correct." They sit thinking and staring out into space and have no basis for forming an opinion. She has to ask herself: "Why did you ever consider this? It is your own responsibility, only you can make the decision." But she defends herself with the argument that if it doesn't help her, it is at least important for them, perhaps one of the best lessons she has given, that communists must have an answer for everything that has to do with human beings, absolutely everything,

at which point one of them, the one who never says anything, says that the important issue for a communist is to know *when* to support other people's decisions and *when* to tell people what they ought to do, to know the appropriate point for resistance or support. "And don't you think," he is saying, "that your aversion to helping Marianna stems from the remnants of a morality that you must cast off, as long as you are living in a society that closes all its doors to an unwed, pregnant girl?" Metta looks at him and says: "Now you're thinking." She divides up the newspapers, they drink the coffee they have been given,

get on their coats, go out on the white street, walk toward the center of town

Halvor Børresen is stirring his cup with a spoon at the table between Marianna and Henrietta. Henrietta is the one putting pressure on him: "Is there really nothing you can do at all to help Marianna out of this impossible situation?" He shakes his head: "I am not the one who decides these things, but she can at least appeal the decision." "This is really rotten," says Henrietta, "I have never thought about how rotten it is until now when I have a concrete example in front of me. It is intolerable." Marianna says nothing. She sits there dreading to call her father and ask how it is going with her mother. Finally she pulls herself together: "Thank you. I have to go now,"

"Are you in such a hurry," asks the Social Services Counselor and thinks that he isn't so keen to be left alone with Henrietta just at this point . . .

"I have to call home. Mother is sick."

"You can call from here!"

Of course, she can. She sees the telephone. She walks over and stops to sort of take a deep breath before she goes on with the call. Then she dials the number.

"How is she doing?"

"She's still in bed, but she is calmer."

"Is there anything I can do?"

"It is important for her to have you at home."

"But that's impossible. I have the afternoon shift today."

He says: "Since you weren't at home when I called you early this morning, I contacted the cafe. They said they would get someone to replace you this afternoon."

Everything is arranged before she even has time to think. Everyone is acting on her behalf without asking her first. And her father has called her landlords, and knows everything about her now, and can do whatever he wants. She answers quickly:

"Fine, then I'll come on the ferry that leaves here at one o'clock."

49

At that point Henrietta Brunberg starts carrying the dishes away from the breakfast table. The Social Services Counselor raises one eyebrow while he looks at her, but makes no comment. Henrietta doesn't look up until Marianna shows up all dressed and says: "Thank you for all you've done. I have to stop by my room . . ." And Henrietta asks: "Can't you wait for me? I'll be ready to leave soon, too," but Marianna has to go, out into the cold wind, and to her dark and untidy room. Her body is frozen and she would have liked to have something to eat: But as she sits down on the couch with a book, just waiting until it is time to get on the ferry, she can't help thinking if there isn't someone she can confide in,

Henrietta Brunberg gets on her coat, on top of her long party dress, which looks funny on a Saturday morning, and the Social Services Counselor sees that and remarks cautiously: "Since you insist on going—can I call a taxi for you?"

"I'll walk," she says. "It is no distance to walk, I'll manage easily. I have to get over there and check out. A teacher's salary won't cover a double room at the Ramvik Hotel any more nights than necessary." And she sees that he is standing there scrutinizing her, not in an unfriendly way, but as if he wanted to know more, something that she has no desire to tell him. He just stands there, and she mumbles: "One more cigarette then maybe . . ." She perches on the edge of a chair, disillusioned because he rushes over to light it for her. She will perhaps have to say something in order not to react impatiently, and she starts talking and discovers as she speaks that every word she says about herself is a little step forward,

"I needled my parents into sending me to the teacher's college. Father was dead set against it, but the entrance exam showed that I deserved to be accepted. He couldn't see the point of it, he thought he would get me back right away, knocked up and dumped, just couldn't imagine that I could cope with a strange town in any other way, living in a rented room, he should have known better. But I had found another interest and didn't even look at a man for the first whole year. I had a secret hobby, an unfeminine passion—I was enthralled by history. I beat a path to the library in Bergen to borrow books on history, sneaked home with them and lay reading them far into the night. Some day, I thought, when I have worked for several years, I'll go to the university and study history. Then I came here and wound up with Arve and a child who took all the time I had outside the classroom, until these last few years, when I have been attending a series of lectures in Molde, trying to get back into it, but I just can't concentrate. What was I saying? I wanted to say that maybe now I can manage. If so, it's about time."

And he asks her a second time: "What are you thinking of doing?" And she says, "I don't know," but she knows very well. He stands in the doorway and gazes after her as she goes down the stairs and out of the building, out onto the road,

and with the long party dress swishing around her ankles, sometimes trailing right in the slush, she walks through the streets toward the Ramvik Hotel, and she knows that the people who see her from their windows will have no doubt whatsoever that she has been at a party. She knows there are people who know her, and even more who know the man she lives with. She could have taken a taxi and spared them both, but right now it was more important not to, and she tries to hold her head high. She felt like a high-class whore, kicked out at dawn, and that's how it would just have to be, for once nothing was going to be concealed. The cold wind went through to her shins, and she was not used to drinking, hadn't washed properly either, her face felt stiff and sickly . . . let them stare, just let them stare. Here goes the teacher from Eik Island who is supposed to educate the children to be respectable human beings, and she has spent the night with the Social Services Counselor in Ramvik and gotten herself a man, look at her now! "If I can't tolerate this, I have no place to go," and she comes walking toward the hotel. It is quiet there at this time of day. At the reception desk there is a cheerful, young girl who shakes her head when she asks for the key to the room: "Your husband has it, of course," and she looks amused down at her,

"that long dress on that middle-aged woman," thinks Henrietta, who asks stiffly: "Yes, of course, but where is he?" "He is sitting up there, I think. He ordered breakfast sent to the room not long ago." She tackles the two flights of stairs, thinking that the guy could have the decency to leave now, he ought to be glad she had let him use the room. When she gets to the door she hears music coming from in there and the cleaning girls peek out of all the corners, having already put two and two together. Then she knocks and it takes a while for him to come over and open the door: "Oh, so you did come," he said, "I was just sitting here wondering if you would turn up."

"Couldn't we talk a little later?" she asks. "You can go down to the salon meanwhile. I need the room for a bit to put myself together." He says, "Of course!" and leaves

in the bathroom there is a box with a thin slot in it for used razor blades, she has undressed and is standing in the shower when she discovers it. She shakes the box, it is apparently possible to fish out one of the blades, and she sees the white hand towels hanging around her and the little pad of thin papers to stop the bleeding with. She stands there shaking the little box, when the man writing opens the door a crack and says: "It just occurred to me . . . maybe I should order some coffee for you or something." She stands, quiet as a mouse, with the blade in her hand until his footsteps have disappeared down the corridor, then sees what she is about to do and suddenly hears that they are in the middle of the morning concert on the Norwegian State Broadcasting System in Oslo: a segment from *Tristan and Isolde* pierces the air. No, it is quite out of the question, she is forced to realize, and laugh, and she slips the blade back into the box and begins to put on her make-up.

The man writing is sitting in the dining room at a hotel on the west coast of Norway waiting for one of the women he has created. There is room for her on the other side of the table, a cup and saucer and teaspoon have been put there. "The brown dress," he thinks, "did not look very good. Hope she has something else in her suitcase," and he jots down some extra clothes, things he would like to have her wear this morning when she sits here with him, drinking coffee. But when he sees her coming, over by the reception desk, she has already packed her bag, and is turning in the keys, and he realizes that she has not done what he told her, but looks decent enough anyway—she has put her face in order.

50

Anna-Marja Kretsen opens her eyes in a loft room beneath a new roof and everything, and for the first time has fallen back asleep after waking up in the early morning. She thinks: "It must be the medicine. Now they are capable, if they so desire, of turning out her lights for good, so that she can lie there, and they can inject her body with whatever nutrients it needs, they can pour it into her, and she will press the excrement out when they ask her to." When she sees that Olver, quite by coincidence, has taken out the bed pan, she uses it, because otherwise she would have to get up, get dressed and go outside. And she stares up at the unpainted ceiling above her, the pine boards that are darkening slowly, the figures in the knots, a face or a dog in the wood patterns she has looked at and not seen every morning until this very day. Now she is painfully aware of them and she lies and strokes the bed cover as if she wanted to smooth out the disheveled pattern in the weaving. But it is much too white, as if she were lying in a hospital bed, and she envisions herself lying there. Down on the first floor she hears that the radio is on and that Olver is padding around, a bit heavily, with muted thuds on the floor planks. She would like to have gotten his attention, she wanted to talk to him now, he ought to understand that he should come up to see her, but she cannot allow herself to shout, for that would make him think that she was raving again. Thud-thud, he walks back and forth, and soon afterwards she hears him coming up the stairs. She positions herself with her head toward the wall and pretends to be dozing when he opens the door and comes in,

but then she turns over anyway and looks at him standing there. He has put on a clean shirt with thin black stripes on the white background, and shaved, she sees that, must have just finished, in fact, since he still has a little shaving cream that he didn't get washed off one of his earlobes, and she asks: "What are you so dressed up for? Is somebody coming here because I'm sick? Did you send for a doctor or somebody without telling me? I don't want to have any doctor or anybody else here," and he tells her that it is because Marianna is coming on the ferry from Ramvik this afternoon, that he has called her and it worked out fine for her to come. "What is she coming home for? She has never done anything but make me nervous. But then what difference does that make, I can't go around looking out for her any more," and she turns toward the wall again, while he remains standing on the floor, looking straight ahead. "I thought you wanted her to come home, otherwise I wouldn't have asked her to . . ."

She turns abruptly toward him: "Where are the others? Where are the boys?" And he answers that they are right outside, and that they can come up so she can talk to them, and he goes down the stairs to get them. They come up slowly, walk hesitantly up to the bed, the youngest, the eight-year-old looks at her solemnly and asks her if she is terribly sick, while the one who is twelve doesn't dare look her in the eye, she notices, because he understands that this is not a normal disease, and he can hardly stand knowing what is really wrong with her,

and she says to them: "I'll get out of bed soon," and they disappear from the room. She lies there, straightening the covers, Olver says that in half an hour the ferry will be on its way over, in one brief hour Marianna will be here, "I had best go down and try to put the kitchen in order, do some of the dishes that have been piling up on the counter at least," She sees that he is standing there wavering, and she can't help saying to him: "Don't you have anything to say to me, Olver?" Then he walks slowly over and sits down on the edge of the bed, and maybe she was expecting that he would take her hand, but no, he sat down on the edge of the bed and stroked his newly shaven chin with one hand to see how it felt, and then he speaks to her slowly and looks out into the room, saying "I don't know what I should say to you, Anna-Marja, but has there been any other way to do things, for us, I mean? Where could we have gone?" and she reaches for *him* before exhaustion overpowers her again, and he glides away from her, she watches him

walking down the road, sees his back from the kitchen window, as he walks to the ferry about seven-thirty in the morning, the crumbs lying on his plate still, the little ring of grounds in the bottom of his coffee cup, which after a while makes a thin, brown film around the inside of the cup that remains when the last drop of coffee has been drained, and he goes

down toward the ferry, and she stands at the window and thinks: "You are lucky, fellow, to be able to leave, and not have to face the daily drudgery here, a messy breakfast table, and a couple of kids who need to be prepared to meet the world. He goes

out of the house, he crosses the fjord and he winds up in a basement where a panel of lights starts blinking when a light bulb needs to be changed on one of the upper levels. Then they call for Olver Kretsen, and he comes rumbling up on the elevator and catches a glimpse of the fjord from one of the windows up there, a glimpse of the Eik Island Sound and maybe the tiny pale house among the swirls of forest where she walks around behind

the kitchen curtains she has sewn herself, but where she now lies in the loft and is unable to do her work, her body heavy as lead. She has no watch, but she begins to wonder whether the ferry won't soon have left Ramvik, and whether you can see it, the ferry, out on the fjord. She finally swings her legs over the edge of the bed and tiptoes over to the window, but still the floor planks creak so much that Olver must surely hear it. She sees from the window that the ferry hasn't departed from over there yet, the weather is so clear that one can see straight across the sound, but what strikes her like a flash of lightning is the thin membrane of wet snow and slush that has arrived. Everything around her on the island is white. She looks over at the bed clothes, lying disheveled and warm from her body heat, and she has to clutch her forehead, for the whole house, the whole island, she is thinking, is the white bed her black body is lying on, this woman who has always walked about on Eik Island among the rocky knolls from the time she was a little girl with her finger in her mouth. She sticks her finger in her mouth and creeps down beneath the comforter again and somewhere down there she gets up and gets dressed for school, brushes her teeth so she can taste the toothpaste in her mouth. And all the while she is lying there, floating off into a state between darkness and dreams.

51

And the man writing has a black spot on his field of vision which sneaks from the attic room where Anna-Marja Kretsen is lying to the teacher's house where Brunberg is standing in the bathroom, looking at himself in the mirror with his head pounding and the radio blaring. And he makes his way down to the kitchen where his daughter is standing with her back to him, watching the coffee pot on the burner. She says that she wants to go to Ramvik on the twelve-o'clock ferry, and he says nothing to prevent her, he pours himself a cup of coffee and thinks: "The worst is over." Afterwards he finds his coat and goes out,

"the worst is over," Henrietta says thoughtfully over her coffee cup at the table in the dining room of the Ramvik Hotel, and in a way this is a time for talking to someone, "but you needn't write that down." She gets up and looks at the clock. "If I'm to make the ferry, I have to get going right now." He gets up to say a proper thank you, because he was allowed to use her room, and it dawns on him how little he noticed up there, other than her clothes, that there would be any value in writing about. He is about to ask to have the key back once more, to make some notes about the interior, etc., but when he puts down his notebook to ask her, Henrietta is no longer to be seen. He sees only a stripe of a light brown purse pass like a thin thread through the dining room and disappear up the stairs beside the reception desk.

52

At that moment the man writing is standing by the window in the dining room of the Ramvik Hotel, looking all the way down to the end of the street, the slush has been spread around by the wheels of passing cars, and furthest away he sees the Big Cross silhouetted against all the white, next door to the Bus Station Cafe. There, he thinks, I will let

the Saturday shoppers go with their purses and shopping bags, shivering slightly in the cold wind. And there Metta Nilsen can stand and

THE FERRY CROSSING

offer her newspapers for sale to passersby, in league with a young man from Ramvik High School. A steady stream of people pass her, the glass doors of the cafe open and close again, people have both arms full, loaves of bread, parcels of meat, milk, stop to chat, but only briefly, because it is cold, Metta asks them in a voice loud enough to be heard, most of them walk right on by, others stop to make sure it isn't the Salvation Army standing there selling "The Battle Cry." At the window of the Bus Station Cafe, over his half-drunk cup of coffee, sits the retired postmaster of Eik Island, Karl Magnus Skogmann, at loose ends this morning, just looking at Metta down below. It is taking a long time to get rid of the copies she carries draped over her arm, she walks back and forth to stay warm, it is half an hour until the ferry goes, to Vind Island and Land Island and Eik Island. But out at the end of the island Karl Magnus Skogmann saw that the big, gray boat had returned, and was docked along the boulders that form the shoreline there. He opens his leather satchel, looks down into one of the side compartments and finds the most beloved of all his books there, the current edition of *The Almanac of Norway*. He looks at the charts for the day, the 31st of October, and finds out that the sun will slip beneath the horizon at eleven minutes past four in the afternoon, and not return until around seven the next morning. Eik Island, too, takes part in the rotation of the planet in space. And the next day, he notices, is the anniversary of the establishment of the first Folk High School, Christopher Bruun will be pleased, hanging there on his wall, and more than one hundred years have now passed since the first protest against dead schools and dead knowledge. Nevertheless, Skogmann thinks that he will have to give up the secretary's position on the board of the Folk High School at the next annual meeting. He doesn't have the energy to continue, the past few days have robbed him of sleep, he can feel the fatigue in his whole body. He thinks about what he will do when the day comes that he no longer will be able to put on the coffee pot for himself there in the postmaster's house. Then they will fetch him and take him across the fjord to the old folks' home in Ramvik, so he can sit there and watch the ferry in the Eik Island Sound, white wreath around the bow, waiting out the last years of his life. Being cared for by others, a washcloth with luke warm water pressed against his old face in the mornings, and a quiet room where he will sit, no tobacco smoke, no music, an imperceptible transition to that great silence, but is that the worst thing that could happen? NO, the worst would be if he lost the perspective he has had since he was young, for a man of his age cannot afford to change philosophy, it is too late to begin to believe in something else, as long as his eyes and interest still focus on the contemporary world. He has always believed in human change, that one by means of the open school could create a human being who would change the world, that is how youth should be, has always believed that everything which, in this phase of life, is scrambled and incomprehensible can fall into place when those who have learned to govern this "land of sloping rock" are given a chance, for our country is rich enough if the resources are used properly. But in the book on social-democratic perspectives there is no room for the people as the true aristocracy. In that book freedom and democracy are seen as technical tricks that get people to believe that everything, absolutely everything is as it should be, don't they see there is no use trying to squelch something that is seething beneath the skin and has to be released or at least eradicated periodically with tablets in small bottles, little white specks that gleam in the hand when one gets them out to swallow them? He gives up the social-democratic perspectives and thumbs further in the almanac, comes to the section on "The Stars as Seen from Earth." For Skogmann there is no other place to see them from. He reads and tumbles into a strange sentimentality he cannot control, as the clock ticks slowly toward the ferry departure. He reads

"Nearly all the approximately 3000 stars we observe in the sky on a clear winter evening are our neighbors in space: along with the sun and hundreds of millions of other stars they form the tremendous galaxy we call the Milky Way System." (Here Skogmann gets up with the almanac in his hand, it is time to go.) "The central mass of stars in the Milky Way System appears as a bright band of varying breadth, the Milky Way, which extends as a continuum across the entire sky. Through large telescopes the band can be seen to be myriads of distinct stars. The reason the stars appear to have this distribution is that our galaxy is in the form of a discus, and that we observe it from a point which lies within it, near the central plane,"

standing there he sees the roof of the Ramvik old folks' home where his universe is going to end, he sees himself as a gleam of light in a discus tossed long ago, will it soon disappear, far out in space, and he wraps his coat tightly around himself and goes slowly down the stairs with the

THE FERRY CROSSING

satchel pressed close against his body, then he opens the door, and the biting wind forces its way through his clothing, a girl stands with her back to him, offering a newspaper for sale, he comes closer and stands and looks, as

Marianna Kretsen, with her hands deep down in her peacoat pockets and nothing to carry, comes walking up to Metta Nilsen and a friend of hers and sees Skogmann standing by the door of the Bus Station Cafe, watching Metta who stands there calling: "The Class Struggle!" to people passing by. He does not see Marianna when he finally dares to go up with a one-crown piece and puts the newspaper under his arm and starts to go toward the wharves.

Just then Marianna runs over to him and says: "Are you going over on the ferry, Skogmann?" He stops and looks at her in confusion, but cannot manage to hide his purchase, and he says: "Uh, yes, as a matter of fact."

53

And Marianna Kretsen has a girlfriend who walks back and forth in the wind asking people if they want a newspaper. She buys one herself and opens it up so the pages billow obstinately. She catches sight of the large headline about elective abortion on the center pages and a sinking feeling overtakes her.

"Maybe you could come with me and sell the newspaper on Eik Island, Metta. Could you?"

Metta Nilsen can.

Skogmann stands a little distance away and watches the two girls who are such good friends. Whatever will he talk to them about when they get down to the salon and the ferry has to make stops first at Vind Island and then Land Island on this trip?

A couple of cars come and get in position to drive aboard. People arrive, wanting to spend the weekend on the island, a little island just off the coast, where a large gray boat has lodged itself and is conducting research.

Karl Magnus Skogmann is standing with Marianna Kretsen, waiting for Metta Nilsen to come back from the tobacconist's shop; she had to get herself some cigarettes there,

and here comes Henrietta Brunberg with her suitcases walking down toward the ferry on her way home to the island, emerging from the gap between the Big Cross and the Bus Station Cafe. She sees the three of them there, Skogmann and the girls, and says: "Looks like people are starting to gather."

"So you've been to town," says the old man to her. "Shall we go right on down to the ferry? I think the girls are cold." And they start walking down toward the ferry where the engines are already running, and Metta says a few words to the fellow she had with her, before he disappears among the buildings in Ramvik. And Henrietta says:

"No, I was going off to war, but I realized that there are a few things I have to finish up on Eik Island first,"

they duck their heads, one after the other, as they go down into the salon on the ferry, for the door opening is too low, but it is warm and nice down there, the whole boat is vibrating and they are underway, while Henrietta opens up Karl Magnus Skogmann's newspaper and sees the coverage of the place where they live, and she turns to him and says: "We don't want any part of this now, do we?" He answers: "We ought to do something to stop them."

And she hears Marianna say to Skogmann that Metta, too, was a student at the Folk High School, but he doesn't pursue the topic.

54

and the man writing gets up from the table at the Ramvik Hotel, and thinks about what his book is going to be about. But outside, sauntering through the streets of Ramvik toward the Big Cross, he sees the ferry far out there, on the way from Vind Island to Eik Island, and he is not at all sure that the people sitting in the salon on board have even noticed the two stops along the way, they are so busy talking to each other. The ferry is running at any rate, and people make their crossings.

THE FERRY CROSSING

At the dock on Eik Island the storekeeper is waiting for a shipment of canned goods, nuts, oranges and chocolate. On his wall a new movie poster has appeared, with pictures from another story, but he doesn't pay any attention to it. What can the man writing possibly assume, other than that they go ashore, and that Skogmann says to Metta that he would like to talk to her about a few issues, and she says that she has time for that, Henrietta turns to him and says that she is coming back down to his place as well, and then hurries off without her suitcases, up the hills to the teacher's house, which lies at the end of the stubby road, goes in and finds the house empty, but tidy after the fellow who has gone out,

And Metta Nilsen and Marianna are on the way to Olver's house, where they go into the entryway and Metta whispers that maybe it wasn't such a good idea for her to come just now. But in the kitchen Olver Kretsen is sitting at the table along with another man, and they are writing up names on a list with a pencil, names of people on the island they can count on for a protest against their being chased away from there, it's Arve Brunberg doing the writing and the two of them walk mentally from house to house and put parentheses around the ones they aren't sure about. And Olver Kretsen getting up and asking the girls to make themselves at home: Marianna looking around, asking: "Where is Mother?"

And she goes up the stairs to the second floor where her mother is lying in bed, running her hand over the comforter, but sits up when she sees Marianna come in and asks: "Who is that talking downstairs? Did you bring someone with you?" Marianna sits down on the edge of the bed, opens her mouth to ask how it is going with her, but notices suddenly that she can't use that approach, takes a deep breath and says quickly: "I have gotten pregnant by a man I no longer care about, and I want to talk to you about what I ought to do."

Dawn begins to break somewhere or other in Anna-Marja Kretsen's head and she says: "Can you get me a wash basin and some water and a comb, so I can fix myself up a bit,"

Marianna goes after these things, and her mother says: "Go downstairs, I'm coming down now, too," and Arve Brunberg is sitting down in the kitchen, winding up a list of names, and there are a lot of them there, and the telephone ringing from down at Karl Magnus

Skogmann's place to say that the girl who came along on the ferry can stay with him, if it is crowded up at your place today, and Olver will talk to her about it. Arve Brunberg says: "I am going down to talk to Skogmann about this list."

Maybe Anna-Marja Kretsen will come down the stairs from the loft just as Brunberg is walking out the door, and say to Olver: "I better get some food made for these girls," and he will notice that she has fixed her hair and put on her Sunday dress, and say: "Food is probably just what they want, Anna-Marja."

Arve Brunberg walks toward Karl Magnus Skogmann's house by the ferry dock. He unfolds the list and smoothes it out on the table, and while the old man reads through it, muttering the names softly, one by one they become real to Arve Brunberg:

Harald Steinen, Amanda Steinen, Nils Ludvigsen, Johan Larsen, Olver Kretsen, Anna-Marja Kretsen. Anna Krokstad, Jørgen Strand. Lars Strand. Theodor Bekk, Elise Tønnesen, Sigurd Seter, Johanne Tønnesen, moving from farm to farm in this manner,

Rikhardt Eikøy, Karl Eikøy, Margaret Johansen, Arve Brunberg, Henrietta Brunberg,

at which point the outer door of Karl Magnus Skogmann's house opens, there is someone in the entryway and Henrietta knocks before she appears at the inner door

Skogmann heads for the kitchen and says: "I better see about putting on the coffee." Henrietta and Arve stand facing each other in the middle of the room. She says: "I have been home, noticed that you had cleaned up after yourself."

He says to her: "You came back today, all right, but what are you thinking of doing now?" And she answers that she has been thinking of resigning her job in the spring, because she wants to go to Oslo for a while and finish her study of history, "the studies I gave up on about twenty years ago. But first of all there are some things I have to talk to you about,"

and Olver Kretsen comes into view in the doorway, along with Metta Nilsen, while Skogmann sets the coffee cups on the table in the space he has cleared by shoving his books to one side, and they sit down there by the window and now the ferry has long since returned to the dock in Ramvik, while Skogmann wants badly to tell a story, about the island they are on, a little island, Eik Island, no more than one and a half kilometers long, off the west coast of Norway, with windblown clusters of trees scattered about and fish in the sea beyond. A story about the telephone and electricity cables that were stretched across the fjord and the lumber that people brought across the Eik Island Sound to put up houses here—a post office, now closed down, a few dilapidated community buildings and a store. And people who walk around and the small flocks of sheep that will be rounded up and brought inside on this day, since it looks like the snow will be coming earlier than usual.

Marianna Kretsen has been talking across the fjord by telephone, and her mother, who is standing in the kitchen waiting for her, hears her say "Goodbye" softly before she puts the receiver back on the hook.

55

The blue bus stops and picks up the man writing at the Bus Station, he hands over the money for the ticket and recognizes the face of the driver, one of the ones he met last night, and Fredrik, who takes his money, says only: "You're on your way home now," and he drives off toward Molde, where

Hans Kristiansson pays for a long distance call to Eik Island in the lobby of the Alexandra Hotel and walks, all dressed up, into the salon where a black suitcase is standing next to his table and his coat is hanging over the chair. It is nearly two o'clock and the regular Saturday lunch guests are beginning to arrive. His hand trembles ever so slightly as he lifts his half liter of beer, that fellow Hans Kristiansson, notes the man writing as he walks in the door, and Hans catches sight of him and beckons to him to come over and sit down.

"You on your way to Oslo now?" Hans Kristiansson asks.

The man writing nods:

"Will we be travelling companions?"

"Yes, I have to disappear for a while," says Hans, "I don't know for how long. There are several things I have to straighten out, which I can't take care of here."

"And Marianna?" the man writing asks.
"I have written to her. A letter."

And the man writing tries to create the letter, but can't do it. He boards the Braathen Airlines jet late that afternoon and finds a seat on the left side of the center aisle, so that he can follow the outline of the coast as the plane turns northward for the stop in Kristiansund. He floats above the chaotic stretch of coastline and sees, between the other holms and islands, a little piece of land out in the sea, no more than one and a half kilometers long, with wind-blown clusters of trees scattered about and a little stub of a road tossed there with a flick of the wrist. "It just isn't true," he thinks, "that art is a mirror; art is a way of holding a sphere, a sphere of glass, which I am sitting and gazing into,

it is filled with a clear liquid, and at the top a white airplane is floating, at the bottom I see the coastline with Eik Island and Land Island and Vind Island,

and when I put my eye up to it, I can see the ferry at the dock in Ramvik. On the other side of the sound I know Skogmann lives. A shadow passes on the road over there, it may be a human being. It may be Metta Nilsen, walking from house to house."

FRANKIE DENTON SHACKELFORD
Translator's Afterword

EDVARD HOEM, WHO RECEIVED both the Norwegian Melsom Award and the Swedish Academy's Dobloug Prize for his novel *Ave Eva* (1987), is one of Norway's most heralded literary talents today. He writes in New Norwegian, a rural variant of Norwegian that survived in spoken dialects throughout the centuries when Norway was ruled by Denmark and Dano-Norwegian was the standard language of the educated class. First established as a written language in the mid-nineteenth century, New Norwegian has flourished as the preferred medium of literary expression of such great writers as the poet A. O. Vinje and the novelists Arne Garborg, Olav Duun, and Tarjei Vesaas. To this rich linguistic tradition Hoem adds the wider aesthetic range and the sharpened political perspective characteristic of the generation of writers that debuted in the late 1960s. Stylistically, Hoem has alternately eschewed and renewed the dominant tradition of realism and has produced works in many literary genres. He is not only an acclaimed novelist, but a lyric poet, dramatist, theater critic, translator, biographer, and literary theorist, and possibly the most versatile writer of New Norwegian since its official adoption by the Norwegian parliament in 1885.

Hoem was born on March 10, 1949 in a small rural community in the northwestern fjord district of Romsdal and grew up in a poor, but very religious family. His father was a farmer and lay preacher, and from early childhood Hoem was surrounded by the harshness and beauty of the Norwegian landscape and the powerful and poetic language of the Bible and the hymns sung at prayer meetings. The poverty and piety of rural Romsdal in the years following the second world war colored Hoem's view of life, inspired his attempt to overcome his background, and provided the raw material for much of his fiction. Many of his works are set in the rugged coastal region he knew so well from childhood and reflect a dedication to understanding the historical experiences and social conditions that shaped life there.

An avid reader and decidedly intellectual child, Hoem was not drawn to farming and, instead, was sent to school in the nearby town of Molde. There he began writing poetry and associating with other poets and musicians connected with the town's annual Jazz Festival. Hoem moved to Oslo to attend the university and he published his first collection of poems there in 1969, followed by a lyrical novel *Landet av honning og aske* ("The Land of Honey and Ashes," 1970). At the University of Oslo Hoem became very interested in political philosophy and, like his contemporary Dag Solstad, he developed a style of writing in the 1970s that was aimed at illuminating social problems and political history from the standpoint of Marxist ideology. His 1971 novel *Anna Lena* depicts the fate of young people from rural areas who move into towns. It reveals not only the psychological trauma of their transition but the economic and political forces controlling their lives in post-war industrial society. Similarly, his first play, *Kvinnene langs fjorden* ("The Women along the Fjord," 1973) focuses on the debilitating effects of uncontrolled capitalism on the remote areas of Norway. This and subsequent plays have led critics to compare Hoem with Bertold Brecht for his consciously political dramaturgy, a comparison which too easily neglects the influence of the indigenous theater tradition, the effects of Russian experimentalism as mediated by, for example, Nordahl Grieg, and Hoem's own lyrical, visionary stagecraft.

Hoem's breakthrough as a prose writer came with the publication in 1974 of the novel *Kjærleikens ferjereiser* ("The Ferry Crossing"), a collective portrait of an isolated island community threatened with forced depopulation by the government. During the next decade Hoem continued to write fictionalized political history in the novels *Melding frå Petrograd* ("Report from Petrograd," 1978) and *Fjerne Berlin* ("Distant Berlin," 1980), and in the plays *Musikken gjennom Gleng* ("Music All Through Gleng," 1977), *Der storbåra bryt* ("Where the Big Waves Break," 1979) and *Lenins madam* ("Lenin's Madame," 1983).

In the 1980s Hoem emerged as a sophisticated stylist, concerned with the formal aspects of his writing, while turning toward themes and settings at once personal and universal, such as the mid-life crisis of a successful actor in the novel *Prøvetid* ("In Rehearsal," 1984) and in the mythification of his own childhood in *Heimlandet Barndom* ("Childhood, My Homeland," 1985). Hoem's continuing dedication to the explication of Norwegian history through literature is evidenced in both *Ave Eva* ("Ave Eva," 1987), an intricate tale set in modern Norway but spanning generations of intrigue and mystery, and *Sankt Olavs skrin* ("Saint Olav's Shrine," 1989), a historical drama based on events in the sixteenth century.

The Ferry Crossing

On its publication in 1974, *The Ferry Crossing* was awarded the Norwegian Critics' Prize and lauded for its social relevance and its innovative narrative technique. The novel sheds light on a number of issues hotly debated in Norway at that time—sex roles, women's liberation, abortion, decentralization versus centralization of the Norwegian economy, the social welfare system, and the effectiveness of the Labor government. Written just after the historic 1972 referendum in which the Norwegian electorate voted not to join the European Common Market, the novel attempts to expose the political tensions inherent in Norwegian society by presenting them in microcosm in the fictitious community of Eik Island and the nearby town of Ramvik. Widely divergent political viewpoints are displayed in the various characters and their encounters with each other during three days in late October 1970. Near the end of the narrative many of the main characters find themselves gathered in one spot; they engage in conversation that lays bare the problems they have, both social and personal, and the reader shares their insights as well as their bewilderment. They fail to come to any clear conclusions, but they achieve a measure of understanding that allows them to overcome their differences and work for a shared goal, namely the preservation of their autonomy as a community. The analogy of their situation to that of Norway on the outskirts of European society is apparent, but the book's message, as stated by one of the main figures, Karl Magnus Skogmann, has general validity for many cultural and historical configurations: "What happens inside us happens on account of what happens around us. It happens despite our wishes and our hopes." Human beings are social animals and the psychological problems of the individual are inextricably linked to the larger forces of economic and political history.

Despite its historically accurate backdrop and political undertones, *The Ferry Crossing* is not merely another example of social realism. Rather, in its most basic concept, it is a self-conscious work about the process of writing fiction and about the role of the writer in society. Although Hoem sympathized with the political goals of the working class of Norway, he did not perceive his task as a professional writer to be that of generating Marxist propaganda. In a speech made in 1980 Hoem pointed out that "no matter how militant art is, there is always an element of play in it, an element of trial and error, of searching without knowing exactly where one will end up" ("Kunst, historie og marxismens menneskesyn." *Profil* 3/4 (1980): 37). The novel's nameless narrator, referred to only as "the man writing," is introduced to the reader in the midst of just such a playful struggle. In what at first appears to be a traditional frame for his narrative, he returns to his typewriter on a rainy night in Oslo, determined to get his vision of Norway across to the readers. He has found it necessary to "correct" the official map of the country by adding ten new miles of seacoast, including the previously non-existent Eik Island and nearby town of Ramvik, as a setting in which the events unfold. "The man writing" frequently underscores the fictionality of his creation. With a flick of his wrist or a wave of his hand he conjures up his characters and proceeds to push and pull them into action like marionettes. The reader is witness as places and props are written into being, such as when the narrator writes a letter to the ferry service begging them to put up a mirror in the bathroom of the ferry. We observe how events experienced by the writer in the frame of the narrative affect the direction his story will take. When he goes out onto the streets of Oslo and notices people coming out of the theater, for example, he then goes home and writes that the movie has let out in the fictional town of Ramvik.

As "the man writing" moves from one character to another in his carefully composed group portrait he often leaves a sentence unfinished, skips a few lines and picks up the narration in another location with intentional disregard for punctuation and conventional syntax. The spatial arrangement of the text alerts the reader to shifts in perspective, and provides a continual reminder that we are being given bits and pieces of a *constructed* world. This technique resembles in prose the constant interruptions for "Verfremdungseffekt" in Brechtian theater. Ironically, while the reader is thus forced to maintain intellectual distance from the narrated events, the narrator himself is gradually drawn into the fictive world he is creating. As early as chapter three there are indications that "the man writing" is not the sovereign author of the events he is narrating, but rather is merely describing them as a somewhat confused eye-witness. Although he is actually still in Oslo, writing, he feels himself being absorbed into the fiction. Unlike traditional omniscient narrators who tell a tale *ex post facto*, "the man writing" can be observed making up the events as he goes along, taking inspiration from his surroundings, aware that the process is ongoing, forward moving, like history itself. As a writer he is situated within the real world, unable to get outside and describe it objectively. But even a fictional world of his own creation cannot be described from outside.

The complex relationship between art and reality is well illustrated in the novel by the growing inability of "the man writing" to distinguish the realms of his fiction and his everyday life. He is so convinced of the correctness of his version of modern Norway and so eager to "get it right" in his book, that he eventually decides to visit the town of his imagination and observe his creation first-hand. He flies to Molde and checks into a hotel. The people there have never heard of Ramvik, of course (their maps are incorrect!), but luckily he runs into Hans Kristiansson, one of his characters, so he knows he is on the right track. Young Kristiansson, who is consistently portrayed as a scoundrel and responsible for one of the novel's central *social* dilemmas, now functions to illuminate the novel's primary *aesthetic* problem, namely that of the relationship of art to the social context from which it springs.

In an entertaining sequence the narrative framework is broken, the boundary between art and artist is removed, and the painter, as it were, spills onto his canvas. In the key passage showing the mutual interaction of narrator and narrative, "the man writing" sits in a cafe on a mountainside near Molde. In a literal as well as intellectual fog, he is in need of a clearer view of his characters, when suddenly Hans Kristiansson enters the same cafe. The shattering of the frame occurs in the metaphorical description of how an artist takes inspiration from his surroundings in much the same way that a smoker with no matches lights his cigarette from the last glow of another person's and then returns the favor later on when his own cigarette is nearly out. Hans Kristiansson comes over to the narrator's table to bum a cigarette from him and they strike up a conversation. "The man writing" asks to catch a ride back to Molde with him and becomes the victim of a practical joke perpetrated by this character of his own creation. As readers we are amused, but also confused. Is the fiction real, or is the narrator fictional? By the end of the narrative, the alleged writer has lost all control over his characters. He is incapable even of composing a short letter from one of them to another.

The outcome of the various social and political debates for which the narrator has served only briefly as midwife will not be his to decide. He has initiated a process, rather than exhibited a finished product. In a final reflection on his role as artist, "the man writing" concedes that "it just isn't true . . . that art is a mirror; art is a way of holding a sphere, a sphere of glass, which I am sitting and gazing into." By holding his eye close to this glass sphere, he is able to see his entire fictional world, and hovering above it, a tiny white airplane heading for Oslo. Paradoxically, the narrator himself is inside the airplane that is inside the glass sphere into which he purports to gaze.

Of course, "the man writing" is not the author of the novel. He is simply a convenient vehicle by means of which Edvard Hoem parodies the narrative techniques of realism and probes into the function of art in society. Exactly how does the form of *The Ferry Crossing* relate to the work's political message? The fragmented text and the broken narrative frame are typical tools of the deconstructionist writer. By showing the reader how art is constructed, Hoem is inviting us to deconstruct our own reality, to use the insights of literature as a basis for social action. Hoem questions traditional literary form so that his readers will question the forms and conventions of their lives. In the end, the reader is left feeling not that he has been shown a corrected vision of Norway, as promised on page one, but rather invited to create his own perspective.

In order to engage the reader's critical consciousness, Hoem disrupts the surface appearance of the text in a kind of prose equivalent of Brecht's alienation effect. But this was not the primary aesthetic principle underlying the work. An equally potent influence in Hoem's choice of artistic form in 1973 was, as he himself has pointed out, the aesthetic theory of Theodor Adorno. While many Marxists in the early 1970s were proclaiming the death of art in the Nuclear Age, Adorno saw in what he termed "authentic" works of art a unique opportunity for a kind of "unconscious historiography." Only a subject, such as "the man writing," who is willing to put his own being into the work of art can accomplish this, however. Clearly, Adorno did not consider social realism to be a necessary corollary to the materialist philosophy. Instead, he urged modern artists to seek "liberation of form." He perceived the production of art as a twofold process of dissolution and reconstruction, a transformation of reality rather than a photographic reproduction of it. Only by dismantling reality, in Hoem's case through the construction of an opposed fictional world, can we see the hidden forces at work in history.

The constant dialectic between process and artifact, the social and the aesthetic in works of art, is well illustrated by the fate of "the man writing." Having been absorbed into the fiction or "objectified" as Adorno would say, he is no longer able to complete the task of narration. He has, however, succeeded in setting the reader, his silent but constant collaborator, into motion. Just as "the man writing" sees himself inside the fictional world he creates, we as readers must be aware of our location "inside of" history if we are to understand and shape it.

This novel is the first work by Edvard Hoem to be translated into English. I would like to thank Kristin Brudevoll of the Office for Norwegian Literature Abroad for suggesting and encouraging this project and Edvard Hoem for his willingness to answer questions and discuss difficulties in the translation process. I am also grateful to my husband Jole Shackelford for reading and suggesting improvements in the manuscript throughout its evolution and for his invaluable help with word processing. Finally I want to express my appreciation to the American Scandinavian Foundation for awarding my translation their annual translation prize for 1988.

Frankie B. Shackelford
The University of Oslo June 1989

Select Bibliography

Grimstad, Ivar. "Christopher Bruun, Mette Nilsen og Edvard Hoem." *Syn og Segn* 4 (1975): 205–211.

Grøgaard, Johan Fredrik. "Samtale med Edvard Hoem." *Vinduet* 1 (1974): 4–9.

Stegane, Idar. "Samfunn og samliv med Edvard Hoem." *Syn og Segn* 4 (1975): 195–204.

Tjora, Øystein. "Sjølvinnsikt og politisk innsikt i Edvard Hoems romanar." *Norsk litterær årbok* (1977): 125–147.

Some Titles in the Series
JAMES J. WILHELM
General Editor

1. Lars Ahlin, *Cinnamoncandy*.
   Translated from Swedish by Hanna Kalter Weiss.

2. *Anthology of Belgian Symbolist Poets*.
   Translated from French by Donald F. Friedman.

3. Ariosto, *Five Cantos*.
   Translated from Italian by Leslie Z. Morgan.

4. *Kassia: The Legend, the Woman, and Her Work*.
   Translated from Greek by Antonia Tripolitis.

5. Antonio de Castro Alves, *The Major Abolitionist Poems of Castro Alves*. Translated from Portuguese by Amy A. Peterson.

6. Li Cunbao, *The Wreath at the Foot of the Mountain*.
   Translated from Chinese by Chen Hanming and James O. Belcher.

7. Meïr Goldschmidt, *A Jew*.
   Translated from Danish by Kenneth Ober.

8. Árpád Göncz, *Plays and Other Writings of Árpád Göncz*.
   Translated from Hungarian by Katharina and Christopher Wilson.

9. Ramón Hernández, *Invitation to Die*.
   Translated from Spanish by Marion Freeman.

10. Edvard Hoem, *The Ferry Crossing*.
    Translated from New Norwegian by
    Frankie Denton Shackelford.

11. Henrik Ibsen, "*Catiline*" and "*The Burial Mound.*"
    Translated from Dano-Norwegian by Thomas Van Laan.

12. Banabhatta, *Kadambari: A Classic Sanskrit Story of Magical Transformations*. Translated from Sanskrit by
    Gwendolyn Layne.

13. *Selected Poems of Lina Kostenko*.
    Translated from Ukranian by Michael Naydan.

14. Baptista Mantuanus, *Adulescentia: The Eclogues of Mantuan*.
    Translated from Latin by Lee Piepho.

15. *The Mourning Songs of Greek Women*.
    Translated from Greek by Konstantinos Lardas.

16. *Ono no Komachi: Poems, Stories, and Noh Plays*.
    Translated from Japanese by Roy E., Nicholas J.,
    and Helen Rebecca Teele.

17. Adam Small, *Kanna–He Is Coming Home*.
    Translated from Afrikaans by Carrol Lasker.

18. Federigo Tozzi, *Ghisola*.
    Translated from Italian by Charles Klopp.

19. *The Burden of Sufferance: Women Poets in Russia*.
    Translated from Russian by Albert Cook and Pamela Perkins.

20. Chantal Chawaf, *Mother Love, Mother Earth*.
    Translated from French by Monique Nagem.

NORMANDALE COMMUNITY COLLEGE
LIBRARY
9700 FRANCE AVENUE SOUTH
BLOOMINGTON, MN 55431-4399